PATHFINDER
SERIES

The Wreck
of the
Pied Piper

C.N. MOSS

D1562302

ZONDERVAN
PUBLISHING HOUSE
OF THE ZONDERVAN CORPORATION
GRAND RAPIDS, MICHIGAN 49506

THE WRECK OF THE PIED PIPER
Copyright © PICKERING & INGLIS LTD. 1973

Published in 1973

Published by Zondervan Publishing House in the USA by special arrangement with Pickering and Inglis Ltd. of London and Glasgow.

Zondervan Edition 1979

Library of Congress Cataloging in Publication Data

Moss, Charles Norman.
  The wreck of the Pied Piper.

  (Pathfinder series)

  SUMMARY: While on summer vacation, three youths unearth the truth about a stolen jewel on an old wreck when the thief comes back to claim his treasure.
  [1. Mystery and detective stories]   I. Title.
II. Series.
PZ7.M8519Wr   [Fic]   78-23264

ISBN 0-310-37831-1

To Mum and Dad

CONTENTS

1
Outward Bound

"Can't you read?" The blue-jerseyed sailor asked caustically. He pointed to a large notice at the stern of the vessel which said, in bold red capitals: IT IS DANGEROUS FOR PASSENGERS TO PASS THIS POINT.

Tom, who had been hanging over the rail watching the foaming wake of the vessel, came back grinning ruefully.

"Sorry!" he said.

The sailor grunted in disgust and turned away.

Tom had curly black hair and blue eyes. He had a cheerful grin, and a way of getting what he wanted. Being told off by the sailor didn't trouble him at all. Grownups were often annoyed with Tom.

Bernard glanced up towards the top of the swaying mast, where the sea gulls wheeled and circled.

"It really is happening," he thought to himself.

It had only begun to seem real as the boat set sail. The engine room telegraph had tinkled sharply. White foam churned away from the stern of the steamer. On deck the sailors had stowed away the mooring ropes with swift efficiency. To them, as to the Captain on the bridge, this was just another morning trip to the Is-

1

lands. To Tom, Bernard, and Jill, it was the beginning of adventure.

The gap between the steamer and the wharf had widened rapidly. Soon the boat was rounding the entrance of the harbor. One or two holiday-makers were by the odd stunted lighthouse that stood at the mouth of the harbor. They had waved to the steamer, and Jill waved back. The next moment the ship had begun to roll. They were no longer in the protected waters of the harbor. The journey had really begun.

Up till then it had all seemed like a dream. Bernard had written the luggage labels for the trunk himself. He used block capitals, taking great care that the addresses were clear to read: "% Mr. & Mrs. F. Watson," he had written. "Dare Cottage, STORN." It seemed such a short address. No street name. No number for the house. Still he supposed it was all right, for that was the address Uncle Fred had given them.

He had watched his father tie up the trunk with tight and careful knots.

"Mustn't let Fred think that we are landlubbers!" his father had said.

Just before the end of the school year, Bernard had come home from school to find that the trunk was no longer standing in the hall.

During the day the van had called and taken it to the station. By now it would have arrived at Dare Cottage. Yet it was still hard to realize that it was true.

Bernard had been "boat crazy" for years. Auntie Su and Uncle Fred had always seemed wonderful people to him, for they lived on an Island. They had only visited his home on two occasions that he remembered. The

2

most recent visit was just about a year ago. They had made a great fuss over him and his sister Jill.

Uncle Fred's face was tanned by the sun and the wind, and his eyes were shrewd and humorous. He talked quite casually of the cabin cruiser that he owned, and of sea fishing, and of the wrecks that used to happen in the old days.

Bernard longed desperately to visit the Islands. "Do let's go on a vacation there, Dad!" he begged.

His father had not been encouraging. "The trouble is to find the money, Bernard. The train fare is expensive, and then on top of that is the fare on the steamer. I just don't see how we can afford it."

Bernard had given up hope. Then a few weeks before the summer vacation the invitation had arrived. Would Bernard and Jill like to spend the holidays at Dare Cottage? Wouldn't they just! Better still, Auntie Su's letter went on to suggest that they might like to bring a friend, as well. Tom's mother was recovering from an operation, and it was agreed that he should go.

Jill was the only drawback to the vacation, as far as Tom was concerned. He and Bernard were great pals. It seemed a shame that their adventure was going to be cluttered up with Bernard's sister. However, as they got to know one another on the long train journey he decided that she was O.K. Like Bernard, she was quiet, and she seemed willing to do as she was told without getting in the way.

By now the steamer was out of the shelter of the mainland, and beginning to feel the force of the Atlantic breakers.

"Just look at that, Tom!" said Bernard.

A huge wave had risen like a green wall behind the stern and crashed down upon the deck.

"You would have been washed overboard if that sailor hadn't called you back."

"I would have dodged," retorted Tom.

"Dodged, my foot," said Bernard scornfully. "At any rate, you would have been soaked to the skin."

"I never knew you cared!" Tom said, grinning. "Dare me to go back again?"

"Not on your life. Let's have another look around the ship."

After the first hour and a half, time began to hang heavy on the hands of the trio. They had explored the boat from end to end. The boys spent a long while peering down into the engine room, watching the mighty movement of brass and steel, and sniffing the distinctive smell of hot oil and metal.

They explored the various rooms and returned to the top deck. Tom's mouth was stuffed with candy.

"Want a bite?"

Jill, who had not been down below, shook her head sharply and said nothing.

"You look a funny color," said Bernard. His tone was of agreeable interest rather than sympathy. Jill still had enough spirit to stick her tongue out at him.

"Look," said Tom, "stand near the middle of the deck and try to sway against the motion of the ship like I'm doing."

Jill followed his advice and began to feel a little better. Stewards were inviting passengers to lie down below. But she did not really want to give in.

Her determination was rewarded. For, half an hour

4

later, she was the first to spot on the horizon something which seemed to be a long low bank of cloud.

"What's that?"

"I think it must be the Islands," replied Bernard.

Steadily the outline grew clearer as the steamer forged through the waters. As they came nearer they could see the Islands lying like green gems in a sea of sparkling blue.

A small crowd had gathered on one side of the ship. A sailor was pointing out various landmarks. Tom squeezed his way into the crowd.

"Which is Storn?" he demanded.

The sailor pointed. "That rugged one farthest away from us."

Tom hung over the rail trying to make out as much of the scenery as he could. His thoughts were full of swimming and boating, fishing and exploration. He little thought what danger and fear they would know before the vacation ended.

2
Arrival

The steamer was quite close to Main Island now. It was easy to pick out the houses. For the most part they were low, gray, weather-beaten cottages. Built of stone, their roofs were made of iron gray slates held in place with cement. Many were surrounded by their own patches of cultivated ground. Here and there men were busy in the fields. A herd of cows was grazing near the shore.

Suddenly the steamer sounded her siren. Jill nearly jumped out of her skin. It was an ear-splitting noise.

"The whistle is spitting," complained Tom. Sure enough, hot drops of water sprayed down on them. Then the vessel began to turn, and as she entered the calmer water between two islands the rolling motion ceased.

Bernard began to feel butterflies in the pit of his stomach. By nature he was shy, and he hated talking to strangers. He knew that the steamer would dock at Main Island. To get to Storn, they would have to book their passage on one of the small ferry boats. He would have to see to getting their luggage transferred from the hold of the steamer to the ferry.

That meant quite a lot of arranging things.

Of course, Tom could do it. Tom had never discovered what shyness was. For that reason Bernard was determined not to ask his help. After all, he was the host. He would have to do it. Bernard had hoped against hope that Uncle Fred would come down to meet them. But in his letter Uncle Fred had explained that he could only get down if the tide was right. He had given careful instructions about the ferry boat, and it seemed pretty clear that he did not expect to be down himself.

Looking up channel between the Islands, Bernard could see a whole crowd of launches with their bows towards Main Island. Judging from the way in which each boat was nosing into the waves, and churning up a wake, they were all in a hurry to meet the steamer. Bernard wondered whether Uncle Fred's cruiser was among them. It would complicate things even more if he paid for tickets on the ferry, and then found that Uncle Fred had turned up after all.

As the steamer rounded the headland, the wharf and floating dock came into view. The wharf occupied one side of a bay which formed a natural harbor. In the bay any number of small craft rode at anchor. The majority were smartly painted in bright colors.

"All shapes and sizes," commented Tom. "Which one shall we use?"

"That one!" said Jill, decidedly. She pointed to the center of the bay. An ocean-going yacht lay at anchor. Her sails were furled. Her white paintwork gleamed and glistened in the bright sunlight. The decks were a rich mahogany color. Her rails and portholes glinted silver.

8

"Can you see her name?" Bernard asked.

"Yes," said Tom, pointing. "There it is—the *Pied Piper*." Bernard took a notebook from his pocket, and resting it upon the rail of the steamer he wrote the name at the end of a list of names he had been collecting.

The clang of the engine room telegraph, and the changed note of the engines recalled them to the fact that they were nearly at the end of their journey. With engines hard astern the steamer sidled towards the wharf. Almost as soon as she touched, the sailors began to put out the gangplanks. The next moment the first passengers were hurrying ashore. The crowd was so dense that obviously it would be some minutes before Tom, Bernard, and Jill could edge their way through.

"Look, Bernard!" said Tom. "I think somebody wants us." There in the crowd at the bottom of the gangplank was Auntie Su. Inwardly Bernard sighed with relief. No need to worry about the ferry. No need to worry about the luggage. No need to worry about anything. The sun seemed to shine even more brightly for him.

As it was impossible to shout above the noise and bustle of the wharf, Auntie Su contented herself with sign language. The signals were plain enough, however. They were to remain where they were.

They waited patiently until the crowd at the gangplank began to thin out. At the first pause, Auntie Su came hurrying up the plank.

"Have you got your suitcases?" she asked.

"I think they are still below," replied Bernard.

"Well, we had better hurry down and get them." She led the way down through a hatchway, and along the

9

lower deck. A winch was at work. Looking up through a rectangular hole above their heads, they saw a crane lifting bins full of suitcases and trunks onto the wharf.

For a few anxious moments they thought their luggage was lost. Tom dived into a stack of suitcases. He pulled bags this way and that. Near the bottom of the pile they discovered their own suitcases.

"Catch," Tom yelled. Tom seldom passed an object by hand when it could be thrown.

"Did you get the trunk all right?" Bernard asked.

"Oh yes," said Auntie Su. "It is cluttering up my kitchen at this very minute," but she smiled as she said it. "Now look sharp and follow me," she continued.

Instead of going up the stairway, she walked along the lower deck. There they found Uncle Fred. He was resting his arms on the rail of the lower deck, and looking into the steamer from outside.

For a moment Jill thought he must be standing in the sea. A second glance soon explained things. Uncle Fred was standing on the top deck of a beautiful cabin cruiser. He was using his body as a sort of mooring rope to keep his craft alongside the larger vessel.

"Welcome to *Puffin,*" he said. Reaching over he took the suitcases as Bernard passed them to him. In a few moments they were all on board.

"Now, Bernard," ordered Uncle Fred, "you stay up here and fend her off until we are under way."

Uncle Fred dropped down from the upper deck into the cockpit. Tom, sitting in the stern with Jill and Auntie Su, had a good view. The engine was already running. The controls were evidently intended to be worked by hand, but Uncle Fred used his foot. This

10

meant that he could look over the top deck and see where he was going.

"Captain and ship's engineer all at once," he explained to Tom with a laugh.

The steering wheel was joined to the tiller with ropes running through pulleys. This meant that the boat steered very much like a car. Tom watched with eager eyes. He took note of Uncle Fred's every movement. Perhaps he would get the chance to be captain himself before the trip was over.

Uncle Fred twisted a brass wheel on the engine with his foot. There was a swish and bubble from the stern as the propeller began to revolve, and the boat throbbed as the power of the engine was transmitted to the shaft.

Up on the top deck, Bernard felt his feet moving away from his arms. Realizing that the *Puffin* was beginning to move, he pushed hard against the side of the steamer. For one anxious moment he thought that he would not be able to push hard enough. He had visions of badly scratched paintwork. The next minute the bow of the *Puffin* was turning away from the steamer, and with a final push from Bernard they were away.

It was a most marvelous feeling to be standing on the deck. He was no longer an envious tourist watching others enjoy themselves. This was really happening to him. He felt the wind on his cheek as the boat emerged from the shelter of the steamer's great bulk. Then they were clear of the shelter of the harbor, and the boat began to lurch and roll. He clutched the rope firmly in one hand, and with the other gripped the mast. Even so, he had a hard job to keep on his feet. He managed to take the few steps to the windshield, and grasping that with one hand, he felt with a cautious foot for the first of the steps down into the cockpit.

As Bernard dropped down behind the windshield he was amazed at the change of atmosphere. On the deck the wind had been whistling in the rigging and his hands had been cold. In the shelter of the cockpit it was warm, and the engine was giving out a strong oily smell.

Tom had already managed to persuade Uncle Fred to let him steer. It had taken him a moment or two to get the feel of it. The boat's bow turned in the same direction as the wheel.

"It isn't the same as steering with a tiller," Tom explained above the noise of the engine. "With a tiller, you have to push it the opposite way. This is just like Dad's car, only it's slower to respond."

Uncle Fred left Tom and Bernard in charge of the helm, while he fiddled around the engine with an oily rag.

"That is Bugh." Auntie Su pointed out a low-lying island. "It used to be inhabited. Look. You can still see some of the old cottage walls. It looks all right at this time of day. At night, when the tourists have gone, it is an eerie place."

Uncle Fred came out of the cabin carrying mackintoshes and a waterproof canvas.

"Cover yourselves up with these," he said.

Jill thought it rather strange, when the sky was clear, and the sun shining, but she did as she was told.

No sooner had she and Auntie Su got the canvas tucked around them, than the first wave broke across the deck.

The *Puffin* had reached the open sea between the Islands, and was now unprotected from the Ocean rollers. As she pitched and tossed, the waves began to break across her bow, and spray splashed over the windshield, drenching the stern of the vessel.

"Go into the cabin if you want to," Uncle Fred advised the boys. There was not a great deal to be seen inside the cabin. There were two berths, one on each side. Above the berths were portholes through which one could see the sky one minute, and the green sea the next, as the boat rolled. A sail was rolled up on one berth. Every movement of the boat seemed magnified. The whole cabin felt as though it was lurching back and forth. The smell of the engine was very strong.

"I won't be able to stand this much longer," Bernard thought to himself grimly.

At that very moment Tom unashamedly dashed for the door. Bernard was glad enough to follow. Ducking his head he passed through the narrow doorway, and blinked in the sunlight.

"I don't like the cabin myself," admitted Auntie Su. "I would far sooner stay out here and risk getting wet."

The rough seas did not last for long. The rugged grandeur of Storn loomed before them. Eagerly they peered over the windshield. Here and there were little stone houses. They saw a long wooden building which Uncle Fred said was the school. On the brow of one of the hills stood a chapel.

"Can you handle a boat hook?" asked Uncle Fred.

"I'll try," replied Bernard.

"Right. Get up on the deck with it. When you see the

13

buoy floating in the water, pick up the buoy with the hook, and then hang on till I get there. Don't miss if you can help it. Very bad seamanship if we have to do another circle to pick up the buoy!"

The boat hook was a long pole with an iron hook at the end. Bernard went forward with it. For a few moments he stood, feeling rather like a sentry challenging the unknown with a fixed bayonet. The sway of the boat, and the feeling that he must look rather conspicuous, made him lower the hook. He found a small metal roller on the bow of the *Puffin* with a sort of a guard into which the hook rested quite comfortably.

Uncle Fred slowed the engine. The bow wave became a gentle ripple spreading out over the still blue water of the bay. Even in this tense moment Bernard noticed the amazing clearness of the water beneath him. He could see stones lying on the sand below. They seemed to move and twist as the water above them distorted his vision.

Suddenly the float loomed up. It was made of a number of squares of cork, with a rope through the middle fastening them together. On the top piece of cork was a number painted in blue paint.

Bernard made a frantic jab with the boat hook. For one horrible moment he fumbled. Then somehow he managed to get the hook around the rope beneath the surface of the water.

Even as he began to haul in the cork, he heard the engine go into reverse. Then it cut out altogether, and Uncle Fred was beside him on the deck.

14

3
Settling In

Uncle Fred and Bernard hauled together on the rope. It had become surprisingly heavy. The reason for this was soon clear. The rope came to an end, and fastened to it was one end of a length of chain. It looked rusty, and the links had worn into each other with the constant movement of the boat at anchor.

It was ice cold to the touch, and numbed Bernard's hands as he hauled at it. The weight was so heavy now that Bernard could not pull in the chain any further. He braced his feet against the deck, but even so, the chain would not budge.

"Let me have it," ordered Uncle Fred. He took Bernard's place and hauled with all his brawny strength. Suddenly, with a rumble, a heavier chain came over the iron roller. Uncle Fred heaved again. Behind the roller, and between it and the mast was a huge iron hook securely fastened to the deck. Between them they hooked the chain over this.

Uncle Fred straightened his back with a sigh of satisfaction. All was now secure. "It would take a bad storm to snap that," he remarked.

A small rowing boat was also moored to the buoy. It was floating quietly beside the *Puffin*. Auntie Su was putting the suitcases into it. She stowed them away under the seats. With a last look around to make sure that everything was secure on board the cruiser, Uncle Fred swung himself over the side into the small rowing boat. He always called this boat a "skiff." It was nothing like "skiffs" which Bernard and Tom had seen on the river at home. Jill described it as "square at both ends." This made it difficult to tell which was the bow, and which was the stern.

Uncle Fred held the skiff steady. Jill climbed in. It was rather frightening. The skiff was like an eggshell on the water. It lurched alarmingly as she lowered herself into it. By the time the boys were in as well, the water seemed almost up to the gunwale. She held her breath every time the skiff rocked.

As Uncle Fred handled the oars, Auntie Su began to point out the various landmarks. The boys soon spotted a wrecked vessel caught among the jagged rocks at the northerly tip of the Island of Corfulwy. Orange streaks of rust striped its side.

"That happened last winter," said Uncle Fred. "A fearful gale it was. Seas like mountains. We were beginning to think that the days of wrecks were over. It just shows that even with radar and everything else the coast is still dangerous."

"Was anybody drowned?" asked Jill, anxiously.

"Mercifully no," replied Uncle Fred. "We managed to get them all off."

"It was a cargo vessel from Italy," said Auntie Su. "There was a rumor that one of the crew was wanted by the Italian police, but we never heard any more to the story."

Uncle Fred's deft handling of the oars soon brought the skiff to shore. He wore hip boots, and he pulled the boat up the sandy beach until Tom and Bernard could make a jump for the dry land. Then they all pulled together so that Jill and Auntie Su could step out without getting their feet wet.

Bernard helped Jill and his aunt with the suitcases, while Tom lingered to see Uncle Fred pull the skiff further up the beach. He tied the skiff's rope to a piece of chain. Then they hurried to catch up with the others.

The skiff had landed in a small bay. A low cliff surrounded the sand on the landward side. At one place a flight of wooden steps ran up the cliff face from the beach. It was for these steps that Auntie Su was making. From the top of the steps it was a stiff climb through fields and past hedges to the house at the top where Uncle Fred and Auntie Su lived.

The boys were to sleep in a little two-roomed asbestos shack. Jill was to have a room in the bungalow which Uncle Fred had built himself.

While Jill helped her aunt put the kettle on and get a meal ready, Tom and Bernard went to unpack.

The hut had its own front gate, and a little paved walk leading to the front door. The hut had a sun porch, with two small rooms opening off it. There was no electricity or gas, just a candle and kerosene lamp. One room was full of junk. The other was the boy's bedroom. There was not even a water faucet, but just outside the bungalow was a large rainwater barrel. This had a faucet fitted to it at the bottom. Inside the bedroom there was an earthenware jug and a basin.

Tom picked up the jug and sloshed some water into the bowl. The water shot out of the bowl, and all over the washstand, and Tom's trousers as well.

"Steady on!" exclaimed Bernard. "There's not enough water for you to start washing your trousers!"

Tom washed his hands and face in scornful silence. He looked around for a towel. As it was not yet unpacked, he dried his hands on Bernard's best jacket which Bernard had hung on the door.

The short wrestling match which followed ended rather inconclusively. However, when they had gotten their breath back they both felt better, and went on with the business of unpacking.

The trunk was, as Auntie Su had said, standing in the kitchen. They made several journeys between the hut and the bungalow, carrying clothes, swimming trunks, and the various odds and ends which they would need at the hut. Uncle Fred then put the trunk in the loft, and the boys returned to the hut to tidy things up.

It did not take long to unpack. With no mother to supervise, they flung their shirts and pajamas haphazardly into the drawers.

Tom took a box out of his suitcase, and opened it proudly. In it lay a brand-new air pistol, some cardboard targets, and several boxes of slugs.

Bernard whistled through his teeth with admiration. "Let's try it!" he begged.

Tom showed him how to pull up the barrel of the gun. This loaded the spring and revealed a hole in the barrel into which a slug fitted neatly. Then the barrel clipped back into place.

18

Whatever you do, don't touch the trigger," warned Tom. "It's pretty powerful, you know."

They went into the room farthest away from Uncle Fred's bungalow, and pushed up the window. In the field beyond the little garden of the hut, a rusty tin can was nestling in the grass. Bernard took careful aim and squeezed the trigger. There was a satisfying 'clonk' as the slug hit the tin.

"It certainly is powerful," agreed Bernard with a sigh of satisfaction.

Bernard had a slingshot in his suitcase. With it, he had a can of homemade lead pellets. He had found an old piece of lead sheeting at home, and with his father's metal shears he had cut it up into small pieces. Then he had squeezed it into pellets with a pair of pliers and a vise. He didn't normally use the pellets. He didn't know where he would be able to get any more lead. Besides, he knew that they were extremely dangerous. His father had warned him that in a slingshot as strong as the one which he used, they could quite easily kill anyone they hit. Bernard liked to think they were for use in an emergency. Just occasionally he took a shot when he was quite certain that no human being was near.

Tom was already busy throwing off his "town" clothes, and getting into a sweater and jeans.

Bernard lingered over the unpacking of his suitcase. Then, watching Tom out of the corner of his eye, he quietly took out a Bible and put it on the table by his bed. He was ashamed of himself for feeling embarrassed. Tom already knew that he was a Christian. In fact, they often argued about it.

Tom saw the Bible, but he made no comment. Instead he took a comic book out of his suitcase and stretched out on the bed to read it, while Bernard finished unpacking.

In her room, Jill had quickly packed everything away. Now she was sitting by the window filling in the post card which her mother had given her to mail on their arrival. She was feeling a little homesick. Uncle Fred and Auntie Su were very sweet. Their bungalow was the dearest little place she had ever seen. Yet it was not home. Home seemed very far away. She sat and gazed out of the open window. Her throat seemed to be aching.

Suddenly she saw something which made her forget her homesickness. Her window looked out on a field. In the middle of this a lumpy hillock of rock rose to a considerable height. This rocky 'cairn' cut off her view of a part of the field. From behind it a pony came galloping into view. The pony was completely unfettered and moved with the easy grace of a wild creature. The pony's mane was ruffled by the fresh sea breeze. It was completely black, except for the right foreleg which was splashed with white. It slowed down and came to a halt, with its head over the gate which led into the field. Its neck arched in a proud curve. Jill ran out of the house and down the path to fondle and make friends with "Prince," Uncle Fred's black pony.

Auntie Su did all her cooking by kerosene. Some of her neighbors used bottled gas. Auntie Su was quite content with her kerosene stoves, and saw no need to change. A delicious smell was coming from the kitchen. She was cooking a great panful of golden fried potatoes.

Jill returned from talking to "Prince" and began to

20

set the table. It was difficult to find things at first, but by standing and thinking, "Now where would I put that if I were Auntie Su?" she often found the right place without having to ask.

Attracted by the smell of eggs and potatoes, the boys arrived at the bungalow, their mouths watering.

Soon they were sitting around the table. Uncle Fred said grace, and they attacked an appetizing meal.

4
Sunset

In the evening Uncle Fred sat out on the porch with an immense telescope on a wooden tripod in front of him. There was a magnificent view from where he sat.

On one side, the Island ran down to sheltered water. That coastline consisted of curving bays with yellow sands. On the other side, the Island was battered by ocean breakers. The shore was rocky, with huge boulders, rounded by the action of the water, and then granite cliffs.

Out towards the west, immense rocks jutted from the water. Some looked like castles built for giants. Others looked like the fangs of some sea monster.

Down towards the south lay Main Island. The steamer was still moored beside the wharf, waiting for an evening trip home.

"Have a look for yourself." Uncle Fred moved to let Bernard peer through the telescope. First Bernard focused on the steamer. It hardly seemed possible that a few hours ago they had been on board her. Then he looked at the signal tower on the Main Island. He could see the great mast on which a large black ball was hoisted whenever the steamer was sighted coming towards the Islands.

Next he turned the telescope towards Corfulwy. This was the neighboring island to the east. Corfulwy was different from Storn, less rugged altogether, he thought. It had a great deal of cultivated land, and here and there, patches of woodland.

"I don't think I've seen a single tree on Storn," he pondered.

"The weather here is too rough for trees," explained Uncle Fred.

Finally Bernard sighted the telescope down the channel between the Islands. After gazing for a moment or two, he motioned to Tom to take his place.

As Tom took over the telescope, the first thing that he saw was the sight at which Bernard had been looking. There, in mid-channel, between the Islands, in full sail, and seeming to be so near that he felt he could reach out and touch her, was the *Pied Piper*. She was a beautiful sight on that late summer's afternoon. The white water curled from her bow, and her wake gleamed silver gold behind her. Tom feasted his eyes on the beauty of her lines, and the splendor of her snowy sails.

"She only arrived yesterday," said Uncle Fred, in reply to Bernard's question. "They say that her owner is an author. He says he will be around for a few days picking up local color for a thriller he's writing. He does underwater swimming as well—apparently that sort of thing is in the story, too."

"What a life!' Tom sighed enviously.

"We get a good many interesting people here," said Uncle Fred with modest pride. "A few years ago we had

24

a film company making a story about pirates on the Spanish Main. It was almost all filmed between the Islands here."

* * *

Jill was in the kitchen helping Auntie Su with the washing up. She had noticed that Bernard and Tom were missing, and if she had been at home she would have protested by now. However, as it was the first day she decided she would say nothing. She had her own reasons for wanting a quiet chat with Auntie Su.

"Tomorrow is Sunday," Auntie Su said, thoughtfully. "We usually spend it very quietly here."

Jill sensed that her aunt had something on her mind.

"Was that the church we saw when we arrived?" she asked.

"Well, it used to be," her aunt replied. "I am afraid it isn't open any more."

"What is wrong with it?" Jill asked.

"There isn't exactly anything wrong with it, it's just that. . . . Well, your uncle and I are the only ones left who would go. There's no one to preach, you see. Uncle isn't any good at that sort of thing. If you want anything made by hand, Uncle is a real craftsman. He is as brave a hero when he is out in a boat during a storm. But he just cannot preach at all. Besides, what would be the use, with only me to go and listen to him?"

"What do we do then?" asked Jill.

"Well your uncle and I always have a Bible reading, and we pray. Perhaps you would like to join us for that. What about your friend, Tom? Is he a Christian?"

"I don't think so," said Jill, doubtfully. "Bernard says that he isn't. I think they have arguments about it

25

sometimes. But I expect he will do what you want. After all, he is a guest, isn't he?"

"Yes, of course, dear," said Auntie Su. Jill could tell that her aunt was troubled. She continued to wash up and there was a long silence. Jill guessed that Auntie Su's thoughts were far away.

"That is a lovely pony," Jill said at last. She wanted to change the subject, and she also wanted to find out whether her greatest dream could possibly come true. "Does anybody ever ride him?"

Auntie Su's eyes sparkled.

"Now, no hints young lady. Say what you mean plainly!"

"Please, do you think that I could ride him?" gasped out Jill, breathless with eagerness.

Auntie Su smiled down at her. "Well, seeing that you have been a good girl, and you have been working hard while those lazy boys have been peering through the telescope with my lazy husband, I don't see why not." She reached up into the cupboard, and took a few lumps of sugar out of a packet. "However, I think you had better bribe him a little first. You give him these, and when I have finished my jobs in the house I'll come and show you where the saddle is hanging up in the shed."

* * *

Bernard and Tom came to watch Jill spoiling Prince.

"They have sort of family prayers on Sundays," Jill explained, patting Prince on the nose.

"No chapel?" asked Bernard, astonished.

"Not enough people, you see."

"A sensible lot," said Tom. He was deliberately teasing Bernard.

26

For once Bernard was not going to be drawn into an argument. He was too staggered.

"It won't seem like Sunday if we don't go to church."

"Mind you don't say anything to upset them," warned Jill, giving Prince a lump of sugar. "I think Auntie Su is awfully sensitive about the chapel being closed. She almost looked as if she was going to cry when she told me about it."

"Family prayers will have to do then," said Bernard, cheerfully. "If it's any consolation, Tom, I should think it would be much shorter than a service."

"That's good," said Tom. "For one ghastly moment I thought you were going to suggest opening the chapel yourself."

"Don't be silly," said Bernard, coloring slightly. "We couldn't possibly do that. . . ." But his voice sounded a little uncertain.

Auntie Su called Jill in from the field.

"I'll help you saddle Prince," she said. "Uncle Fred is waiting for you, boys. Be sure to put heavy shirts on . . . and boots," she called after their retreating figures.

That evening was one Jill would never forget. Prince was a steady pony, but with plenty of fire in him. His graceful strength exhilarated her. The sea breeze ruffled her hair, and the sun sank low behind the western rocks.

Meanwhile the boys were also enjoying themselves.

Uncle Fred sat contentedly in his skiff and let inexpert hands row him out to his boat. Not to the *Puffin* this time, but to a smaller craft named *Tern*.

Tern had no luxuries like the *Puffin*. She was an open

boat. The engine was housed amidships, and there was a rough wooden bench to sit on. The bilge pump was a homemade affair, a thick piece of wood, with a rag wrapped around one end, worked up and down in a metal tube.

Uncle Fred left Bernard to work it, while he began to get the engine ready. The engine ran on kerosene oil, but it had to be "primed" with gasoline to start it. Great metal thumbscrews were fixed in the cylinders, and Uncle Fred unscrewed these a little, so that he could squirt in gasoline from what seemed to be an oilcan.

"Putter, putter, putter. . . ." The engine spluttered into life.

"That's it," Uncle Fred said with satisfaction.

Tom was tying the skiff to a buoy so that she would be there when they returned. Uncle Fred saw what he was doing and chuckled.

"That's right for Main Island, but wrong for where we're going," he explained. "We're taking the skiff with us this time."

He showed Tom how to fasten the rope to a short post at the stern of the boat. Tom and Bernard watched every knot with great care.

Bernard was still at work with the bilge pump. It was sucking up the water out of the bottom of the boat, and pumping it out through a tube in the side of the boat. Suddenly there was a gurgling sound. Bernard looked over the side, and saw that the steady flow of water was now only a trickle.

Uncle Fred nodded.

"That's enough. No need to do any more." Uncle

Fred came to look over the side. Water was spurting from another hole as well as some steam.

"The water circulates through the engine to cool it," he told Bernard. "We must always make sure that it is circulating properly or the engine might break down. If that happened near the rocks, we'd be in real trouble."

Tom went forward and cast off the anchor chain. The engine changed its note as the propeller began to turn. The skiff, which had been drifting about aimlessly, straightened out behind them. The water churned away from its bow like a speedboat at the seaside.

"I think I like the *Tern*," said Tom. "It's like being on a motorbike, instead of in a car."

"There is more to it than that," agreed Uncle Fred. "There are no decks to clamber over, and not much to knock your elbows on. It is much easier to handle nets and lobster pots with an open boat."

"But what happens if it rains?"

"Well, there is no shelter of course, but we have oilskins in the locker."

As the *Tern* nosed its way towards the southern end of Storn, Uncle Fred began to talk about tides and channels.

"When the tide is low, you can walk from Storn to Corfulwy."

"You certainly couldn't do that at the moment," exclaimed Bernard.

"The tides make all the difference. The lower the tide is, the more careful you must be to keep to the right channel. If you watch a boat, you will see it weave about on the surface for no apparent reason. There are rocks beneath that you cannot see."

29

"Rather like having to drive a car without being able to see the road."

"That's it."

As the *Tern* came out from under the shelter of Storn, Uncle Fred turned her westward. Her bow was now towards the open sea. The change was immediate.

"Go and shelter in the bow, Tom," Uncle Fred ordered. "Here, Bernard, cover yourself up with this raincoat."

The *Tern* battled triumphantly through the waves which came rolling down towards her. Many of them sent spray across her. Sometimes it was as if someone had thrown a bucket of water at Bernard and Uncle Fred.

Tom was undoubtedly in the best position. Where he sat, it was completely protected. The spray missed him, leaving him bone dry.

After a while, he became curious to see where they were going. He raised his head to look over the bow, and was rewarded with a wave full in the face.

He snuggled down lower into the shelter, and contented himself with making faces at Bernard, who had witnessed his ducking with obvious satisfaction.

The *Tern* altered course, and they reached the shelter of one of the uninhabited islands. Quite suddenly they were in sheltered waters.

The last tourists had left this island an hour and a half earlier. The crew of the *Tern* had the bay to themselves, except for the sea gulls wheeling and circling overhead.

The bay was of the whitest sand. The water was so clear that they could see down into the tranquil depths where rocks lay on the smooth sandy bottom, with here and there a patch of dark seaweed. The sun was red on the water. It gave a pinky tinge to the white of the sand. The waves curled gently against the shore.

"Drop anchor," Uncle Fred called to Tom.

"Aye! Aye! Sir!"

The rope ran down into the water, looking like some sinuous snake. The anchor seen through the clear depths looked strangely distorted. Tom watched it plow through the sand, and then tighten against a rock.

Within a few minutes, the skiff was at the shore. The boys tore off their shoes and socks, and rolled up their jeans. They splashed into the water.

"Ouch, it feels like ice!"

The water was tingling and cold. Yet in the light of the setting sun it looked like fire. They dragged the skiff high up the beach, and tied the rope to a convenient rock.

"Always tie the skiff carefully," instructed Uncle Fred. "You never know whether you will be delayed, and the tide may rise. Better safe than sorry."

The bay in which they had landed was of fine sand. It was bounded by boulders and granite rocks. Despite their size, some of the boulders were treacherous. They would shift suddenly beneath a person's feet. Others were as firm as the granite of which the island was made.

"Driftwood is what we want," said Uncle Fred. "Auntie Su does the washing on Monday, and the copper laundry tub boils over a wood fire."

Some of the wood was covered with tar, and small flies had settled in swarms over the tar. But much of the

31

wood was good-looking timber. Sometimes they would find large planks too heavy to be carried.

"You might find a keg of butter," Uncle Fred encouraged them.

"How often does that happen?"

"Well I found one about thirty years ago!" Uncle Fred equipped himself with a long piece of driftwood which he used as a walking stick. The boys followed his example.

Bernard got tar on his hands through making an unwise choice.

"If you do, I shall punch you in the eye," said Tom, sweetly. He had evidently read Bernard's thoughts. So instead of smearing the tar on Tom's nose, Bernard wiped it off on the rocks as best he could.

Tom found a bottle which might have had a message in it, but it didn't.

Bernard found a large can which might have had gasoline in it, but it didn't either.

Apart from these dramatic discoveries, the evening was uneventful.

The party returned laden with wood. The sun was now hidden behind the castle-shaped rocks to the westward. There was a chill breeze. The reds had turned to grays, and the color was fading from the sea. Soon they were chugging their way towards the home mooring. The light was fading rapidly.

Tom fished for the buoy, found it, and hauled it aboard. The chain rattled, and there was a sudden stillness as the engine coughed into silence.

"There's a light on the wreck!" exclaimed Bernard, pointing.

"There couldn't possibly be!" replied Uncle Fred. He looked in the direction of Bernard's pointing finger. "What sort of light?"

"I thought I saw the beam of a flashlight," said Bernard, uncertainly.

"I expect it was someone on the island beyond the wreck," suggested Tom.

"Idiot, there is about thirty miles of sea beyond the wreck." Bernard was scornful.

"It could have been a car headlight on the mainland," Uncle Fred said. "It is amazing how they show up at night."

"Maybe," said Bernard, doubtfully. Inwardly he was not convinced, but nothing further happened to make him suspicious, and the light did not shine again.

The night air was still. They heard the dip and gentle splash of the oars, then the rattle of the driftwood as they unloaded it on the beach.

Jill was making her first experiments at lighting the lamp. It had a mantle, rather like the gas mantles that she had seen in the trailer on their vacation last year.

This was not a gas lamp, however. It had a large container into which kerosene was poured.

"You'll find the meths in the cupboard," said Auntie Su.

Jill opened the cupboard door. A small jar full of methylated spirits had something floating inside which seemed halfway between a wick and a cork.

"Look, it clips onto the tube of the lamp." Auntie Su showed her how to clip it on.

Jill lit a match. The blue flame seemed to clutch at the metal tube like the hand of a ghost. The mantle

33

glowed a little as the flame licked it. "You would hardly have thought that so pale a flame could produce any heat," Jill said to herself. Holding her hand high above the flame, she felt the hot uprush of air.

"As the flame dies down, tighten up this thumbscrew, and then pump a few times," Auntie Su instructed her. "Not too much at first."

Jill was a bit too energetic. A great yellow sheet of flame leaped towards the ceiling with a hissing sound.

"Help," wailed Jill.

Auntie Su swiftly undid the thumbscrew. The flame disappeared as quickly as it had come. She coaxed the lamp a little. They heard a gentle hiss, and a "plop." Suddenly the mantle glowed with brilliant incandescent light.

At that moment cheery shouts sounded from outside. The mariners were home from the sea. Their faces were pink, whipped by wind and sea. Salt was drying in crystals on their hair.

The hall of the bungalow was a welcoming place at night. Its walls were of varnished wood. It was almost like a boat itself. From the ceiling a little red lamp, with a kerosene wick, hung on chains. It gave a warm flickering light.

Auntie Su was heating cocoa in the kitchen. Bread and cheese had never tasted as good as they tasted that evening.

5

On Board the Pied Piper

Sunday was a disaster. All three were tired after the trip. Jill had a headache. Bernard had a hard time getting his eyes to open. Tom was equally tired, but the effect was to make him twice as lively as usual.

Uncle Fred and Auntie Su did their best, but although the finest uncle and aunt in the world, as Jill commented later, they were not altogether used to young people around the place.

"We shall have family prayers at eleven," Auntie Su announced firmly after breakfast.

Tom let out an audible groan. Uncle Fred did not say anything to indicate that he had heard Tom, but neither did he smile.

"You might show some elementary good manners," said Bernard, reprovingly, when they were alone in the asbestos hut.

"I get fed up with religion," said Tom, venomously. "They call it a free country! And look what it does to you. Most of the week you're a decent enough guy, come Sunday you reach for your halo, polish your shoes, and turn into a stuffed dummy. It's like one of those television plays where people get taken over by a force from outer space."

"Christianity isn't like that, really," said Bernard, earnestly.

Tom rolled his eyes heavenwards.

"There you go again," he said, disgustedly. "Oh, the joy of being a Christian! Oh, the blessed rapture!" He began to dance around the small room bellowing, "Joy, joy, joy," at the top of his voice, and banging an imaginary tambourine.

Bernard, whose progress in sanctification was not as great as it should have been, tripped him.

By the time Bernard had finished holding a cold wet wash cloth to Tom's nose, and the bleeding had finally stopped, they were nearly late for family prayers.

Auntie Su had a collection of Bibles arranged on the table. They were of all shapes and sizes, and in varying states of repair.

Tom contrived to allow most of Psalms and Proverbs to flutter across the floor out of his copy.

"We will read around in turn," Uncle Fred announced in a voice that was quite unlike his usual pleasant tones.

Auntie Su began. Jill followed. Then Bernard. Tom's verse happened to be long and complicated. He did not understand a word of it, and he read it that way. Of course the others thought he was being deliberately difficult, and Tom himself felt secretly humiliated because he was the only one who had read badly.

Worse was to follow. They all knelt for prayer. Uncle Fred began. Five minutes later, Tom's knees were hurting, and even Jill was fidgeting. Uncle Fred was still praying.

"He's changed into top gear," Tom thought to himself. "I can't think why Auntie Su says he can't preach. By the sound of it, he can't stop. I should think he'd make his fortune. Billy Graham the second!"

When Auntie Su began to pray, a cold fear suddenly gripped Tom's heart.

It couldn't possibly be, he thought wildly. But it was.

For when Auntie Su had finished, Jill began. They were all intended to pray! He felt like an animal in a trap.

Jill's prayer was simple, and earnest, and very brief. Tom, who was more fond of Jill than he would have admitted, might have been touched. But, under the circumstances, his mind was too busy for him to listen.

Bernard prayed.

"What shall I do!" thought Tom, wildly. Then inspiration came to him. From where, he could not tell.

Bernard finished his prayer. Tom cleared his throat and in the best imitation he could do, he pronounced the benediction!

Uncle Fred, who had a book of meditations open at a sermon he had intended to read next, looked startled.

Auntie Su saved the day. "Lunch is at one o'clock," she said brightly, as though nothing out of the ordinary had occurred.

Bernard and Jill, who honestly had not been looking forward to the sermon, slipped guiltily out of the door. Tom followed them without looking back, head high, and a defiant flush on his cheek.

Uncle Fred and Auntie Su were left alone. Uncle

Fred looked grim. Auntie Su began quietly to rock backwards and forwards in her chair. It was not a rocking chair.

A sound which she was trying not to make spluttered suddenly from the corner of her mouth. Then she began to giggle helplessly. Tears ran down her cheeks. "Oh, Fred," she gasped, "oh, Fred, that poor, poor boy. What a mess we made of it. The benediction, the little monkey! Oh dear, dear, dear!"

"I don't see it was all that funny," said Uncle Fred, reprovingly.

"Fred Watson! How can you be so stuffy? You, who set off the firecracker in 'Onward Christian Soldiers' when Mr. Murgatroyd was leading Sunday school."

"That was different"

"Yes, you were just trying to misbehave. Tom has talent."

"Oh, I don't know. Do you remember the frog in the collection bag?"

"Poor Mr. Murgatroyd. . . ."

* * *

Jill had gone to her room and was lying down. Bernard, furious with Tom, and even more furious with himself, was pretending to read a book.

Tom jumped over the stone wall behind the bungalow and found himself on the main street. This was no more than a cart track. As he came over the wall he nearly knocked down a man who was walking by.

"Hallo, who are you?" asked the man, pleasantly. He was a tubby gentleman with a yachting cap and a white turtleneck sweater.

Tom told the man his name.

"Where were you off to in such a hurry?" asked the man.

"I was after a breath of fresh air. Sunday is very boring round here—I've decided to be an atheist!"

"Good fellow," said the portly gentleman, grinning down at Tom. "Now, myself, I always say I'm an agnostic. It's an easier position to argue from!"

"Can I walk down the road with you?" asked Tom, somewhat fascinated by his new acquaintance.

"Of course. Care for a cigarette?" asked the man in the yachting cap, fishing in his pocket.

Tom was tempted. Apart from any other reason, he would have loved to pay Bernard back by strolling past the bungalow with a cigarette in his mouth. But he was not a fool.

"No thanks," he said bluntly. "I don't mind being an atheist, but I don't want to be a dead one."

"Wise man," agreed his friend. "I have often given it up myself. I remember a few years back I gave it up for a whole week."

The road they were following led down to the beach.

"Well, Mr. Atheist, I must go and cook myself some lunch. Perhaps you would care to join me on board the *Pied Piper* this afternoon."

Tom gasped, "Do you mean that's your boat?" he asked, awestruck.

"But of course," said the gentleman. He sounded quite offhand about it.

"Could I really come, sir?"

The man seemed amused. "Why not? I'm harmless. Write books you know. There's not much to see on board, but we might find a bottle of root beer."

"Could I bring a couple of friends?" pleaded Tom, eagerly.

The man shot a keen glance at him.

"I thought you were a refugee!"

"It would be unfair to leave Bernard and Jill out of it," begged Tom, his bad temper completely forgotten.

"All right then. Come down to the beach about three o'clock, and I'll row over for you."

* * *

Tom's meeting with the captain of the *Pied Piper* was the subject of excited conversation at lunch.

Everyone seemed determined to make no mention of the morning's difficulties, and it was apparent that all was forgiven.

"He said Jill and Bernard could come, too!" ended Tom.

"Very kind of him I'm sure," said Uncle Fred. "Well, I don't see that you can come to any harm. . . ."

"You will be polite, won't you?" cautioned Auntie Su.

Tom gazed at her meltingly. "Could we ever be anything else!"

* * *

By five minutes past three they were all on board the *Pied Piper*.

Their host introduced himself as Mr. Danvers, novelist and playwright.

"You must be awfully clever!" said Jill.

"Oh, I don't know. More hard work than anything, you know. What people don't realize is that you cannot just write a book out of your imagination. You have to do things yourself if it is to sound real.

"For instance, the story I am writing now includes underwater swimming. So I have rented some equipment, and tomorrow I shall go lobster hunting around the rocks.

"Even talking to you three helps me. Maybe I shall put you in my next book."

"Now we won't be able to say a word," said Jill blushing self-consciously.

"Hurrah!" cheered Bernard. "Jill is not going to say anything. Hurrah, hurrah! Ouch!"

"Who would like some root beer? Lemonade?"

They sat around with glasses of fizzy drink. The *Pied Piper* rode at anchor. The sun shone down. Life was good!

"What is your novel about, Mr. Danvers?"

"It's a thriller actually. You see that wreck? Well I am putting it in the story. I reckon that one of the crew of that vessel was a thief. He stole a priceless necklace from an Italian collection. He was coming to England to dispose of it. He hid it on board the vessel, and then when the ship was wrecked he couldn't get to the secret hiding place to rescue it. So he comes back to the Islands to recover it. But another gang of villains is onto the secret as well."

"Go on."

Mr. Danvers laughed.

"You must buy the book when it comes out. On second thought, perhaps you had better not. From what I have heard, it will definitely not be the kind of book your aunt and uncle would enjoy. Lots of swearing and gore and all the rest of it."

"Just my kind of book," said Tom, appreciatively.

Mr. Danvers cocked a thoughtful eye in his direction. "Mmm?"

"Uncle Fred said there was a rumor that a sailor on that ship was wanted by the police," said Bernard.

"Really?" Mr. Danvers's tone was casual. "Well they say truth is stranger than fiction. Perhaps I shall unearth some dangerous criminals, and you can help me bring them to justice!"

From the beach a faint call came sounding over the water.

"I think that is your aunt calling to you to go home to eat."

"Thank you ever so much for having us."

"Thanks for the root beer."

6
Midnight Stroll

"Auntie Su," said Jill, the words tumbling out in a rush, "why can't we have a service in the chapel next Sunday?"

Auntie Su, who had been putting sugar into Uncle Fred's tea when Jill asked her question, ladled in a third spoonful without thinking.

For a moment the room was so silent that you could hear the steady hiss of the lamp.

Now that she had launched the idea, Jill did not feel so timid. She went on eagerly, "I could dust the pews and clean the lamps. Uncle Fred could play the harmonium. Bernard could do the Bible reading, and Tom could take up the offering."

"Can I spend it on candy?"

"Oh, do be quiet, Tom. Can't you be serious!"

"Who would preach?"

"I don't think we need to have a sermon," said Bernard.

"It's not a proper service without a sermon," said Auntie Su doubtfully.

"Bernard has spoken to the Bible Class at home," announced Jill proudly.

Bernard turned red up to the roots of his hair.

"Has he though?" Tom was interested. "I guess they never asked him again."

"Well they did, so there!"

"I could read something out of my book of *Sermons by Great Preachers*," Uncle Fred suggested diffidently.

Tom saw a great chasm of boredom opening up before him.

"Tell you what!" he exclaimed. "If old Bernard will preach, I'll give out the hymnbooks at the door, *and* take up the offering."

"Would you preach, Bernard?" Auntie Su's voice sounded almost pathetically eager. Her conscience had never rested easy to think that the chapel was closed on Sundays.

Next Sunday seemed a long way off. It was quite true that Bernard had spoken at the Bible Class once. Besides, he would only be preaching to people he knew, and perhaps one or two Islanders at the most.

"You wouldn't mind if I read most of it?"

"It would be such fun to have the chapel open," said Jill. "I'll do a poster to go on the little bulletin board outside. Can we pick some of the daffodils for the flower vases?"

"There's some plaster down in one corner," said Uncle Fred. "I can easily get up there with a ladder tomorrow. It will be quite dry by Sunday."

* * *

When the meal was cleared away, they knelt again for family prayers. Auntie Su made it plain that there would be no chain prayer.

Tom knelt in a position where he could stare out of

44

the window. A light flashed brightly in the southwest. Three long flashes, then a long pause. Then another three flashes. It was the "bosun" light warning ships away from the dangerous rocks.

When the family prayers were over, the boys borrowed a flashlight and made their way out to their hut. In the distance the lights of Main Island twinkled and faded.

A noise in the air sounded to Bernard like railroad engines running on the line. Then he realized that there was no railroad for miles. It was the surf on the shore. Not the cozy swish that you hear at an ordinary seaside town, but a steady, though distant, roar. For a moment he had the same eerie feeling that comes when you look up into the vastness of space. The Island seemed small, the ocean infinite.

Inside the bungalow, Tom got out his air pistol.

"This place is too quiet; I want an adventure!"

"Not tonight, Tom; it's Sunday."

"All right, when does Sunday end?"

"Midnight, I suppose."

"O.K., you can sleep till midnight."

* * *

The door of the porch stuck. Tom eased it open with great care. Even so, the door creaked.

"Shhh!"

Both boys were wearing sneakers, and they crept along without a sound. At the gate, Tom hesitated. To go to the left would take them past the windows of Uncle Fred's cottage. The gate out of the field was of rusty old iron; it would almost certainly squeak. To their right was a path which ran out to the lane. This had no regular gate, but a wooden hurdle tied in place with rope.

Tom set off to the right. Climbing over the hurdle was tricky, for it was leaning against the wall. Since the wall was built of stones piled one on top of the other, there was every danger of knocking some down. However, they managed without mishap. Tom kept to the edge of the field, and they crept along in the shadow of the walls.

"I hope no one mistakes us for poachers, and takes a pot shot at us!" whispered Tom with relish.

"What is there to poach?" Bernard was scornful.

"Eggs."

"If you are going to make corny jokes, I'll return to my warm and comfortable bed."

Eventually they found their way down through the fields to a spot where they could look across the channel to Corfulwy.

The *Pied Piper* lay at anchor just where they had visited her that afternoon. Although it was late, her portholes were lit up. They could just make out the head and shoulders of Mr. Danvers. He was sitting with his back to a porthole, reading.

"He keeps late hours," said Bernard.

"Do you call this late? The night is young, sonny."

"I knew I saw a light on that wreck!"

Bernard had clutched Tom's arm.

"Where? Yes, you're right," said Tom.

"There it is again. Who could it be? The coast guard? Tourists?"

"It's a ghastly ghoulish ghost, green and luminous, with phosphorescent eyes, and a hideous gaping wound in its head too horrible to describe!"

"Oh, wrap it up!"

The boys stood hidden in the shadows, gazing out towards the gaunt silhouette of the wreck.

They saw the light flash several more times. Someone was obviously on board. It was equally obvious that whoever it was only used his flashlight when absolutely compelled to do so. Something seemed so furtive about it that cold shivers ran down Bernard's spine.

"Could it possibly be smugglers, Tom?"

This time Tom made no attempt to be funny. He was keeping his excitement in check with great difficulty.

"I don't see what they could possibly be smuggling. Something peculiar is going on, that's a cert."

Some minutes went by and during that time they saw no further signs of life from the wreck. Bernard's legs felt cramped.

"Are you cold?" whispered Tom.

"Frozen!"

"Ought we to sound an alarm?" asked Tom.

"They would say we were imagining things. Besides, we're supposed to be tucked into bed."

Tom had no reply to this. He yawned wearily and said, "The show's over for tonight! Let's go home."

"I think we ought to tell Uncle Fred what we saw," said Bernard, when at last they were in bed.

"Well I don't," argued Tom. "He'll only feel he has to do something about it. You know there are no police nearer than Main Island. Uncle Fred will feel bound to get them up here. Either it will turn out to be a false

47

alarm—some fellow mackerel fishing or something—or else if it really is a criminal, he'll get away. Then we'll miss all the fun."

"I still think we ought to tell him," Bernard persisted, doggedly.

"Tell you what!" Tom sounded quite excited. "Why don't we tell Mr. Danvers?"

"Would he laugh at us?"

"Course not! He'd be as interested as we are. These authors are always on the lookout for real life adventure."

"When shall we tell him?"

"First thing in the morning."

7
Council of War

"Look at Moby Dick!" Tom pointed through the window in the direction of the *Pied Piper*.

"Wow!" said Bernard.

They were eating toast and marmalade to round off a hearty breakfast.

Mr. Danvers was standing on the deck of the *Pied Piper* wearing a dazzling pair of satin swimming trunks. They did not really suit him, for he was a big man, and bigger around the middle than the chest. Fully dressed, he looked quite reasonable, but in swimming trunks he looked a little laughable. His body was the shape of a large white egg, and his sunburnt face, neck, and forearms showed up oddly against the rest of him.

Suddenly he dived from the deck into the water. His head appeared above the surface. His black hair was thin, and a bald patch was beginning to appear.

"Why do you say Moby Dick?" asked Auntie Su.

"Great white whale," mumbled Tom, his mouth full of toast and marmalade.

"I didn't know Tom was so intelligent," whispered Jill to Bernard.

"A book at school. . . ." Bernard explained.

"Look at him, though!"

Out of the water Mr. Danvers might look ungainly, but in it he was magnificent. He swam a steady, powerful crawl. The water curved away from his head. His threshing feet left a white frothy wake behind him. His hands and arms moved with an easy grace, but with tremendous power. All three youngsters swam well, but they knew that here was a swimmer who could make them look like beginners.

"He goes like a torpedo," gasped Bernard.

It was an exaggeration, but the man was certainly fast. There was a machine-like regularity in his stroke. He gave no sign of tiring, or of undue exertion.

After a while Moby turned back, and began to swim against the tide.

"This will test him," said Uncle Fred, a little anxiously. "The tide is more powerful than people realize."

Certainly the return journey was slower, but the man gave no sign of distress. His stroke was slightly quicker if anything, and the choppiness of the waves did not seem to worry him. He reached the boat and clambered up a small ladder hanging at the side. His muscles rippled under the flesh, as he pulled himself on board. He toweled himself vigorously, and disappeared below.

"What shall we do this morning?" Jill wanted to know.

"I've work to do," said Uncle Fred, firmly.

"Can we go for a swim?"

"Of course you can, but don't go out too far."

They put their swimsuits on under their clothes, and taking their towels, hurried off down to the beach. It was a first-rate day for swimming, and for diving, too.

50

They swam between the boats, and used the top deck of the *Puffin* for a diving platform.

Mr. Danvers had settled in the cockpit of the *Pied Piper* and they could hear the faint rattle of a typewriter.

"Better not disturb him while he's working," Tom whispered to Bernard.

In the cold light of day both boys felt a little differently about the excursion of the night before. Would anyone believe their story? Perhaps the incident was best forgotten.

Eventually they tired of the sea, and lay down to bake in the sun. Tom measured the distance between the wharf at Storn and the wharf at Corfulwy in his mind's eye.

"I bet I could swim to Corfulwy," he declared.

"I daresay you could. But you would have to be careful of the tide. If it was flowing fast, you would have to do a big half circle to get to Corfulwy. You might easily get swept out to sea, and drowned. Not that anyone would miss you!"

"Charming."

Jill went wading down at the water's edge. The beach was of finest sand. Even so, there were places where rocks projected from the sand. She found some interesting pools. She tried to unstick the limpets from some of the rocks, but they were firmly attached. Short of knocking them off with another rock there seemed to be no way to dislodge them. She thought it would be cruel to try that.

In the end, she wandered back to where the boys were. To her astonishment they were both sound asleep. They had kept the secret of their late-night stroll, so she took their sleepiness to be laziness.

Tom's mouth was open. He was snoring quite distinctly. Jill looked around thoughtfully. Lying conveniently on the bank was an old bowl with a wooden handle which the men used to bale out their boats. She picked it up quietly and strolled down to the sea. She returned with great care, as though she were carrying something very fragile. She positioned herself stealthily and with care. Then "Whoosh"—the bowlful of water caught Tom full in the face, and there was enough left for Bernard, too.

The boys spluttered and coughed. It took them a moment or two to get their bearings. They wiped the water from their eyes, and tried to make out what had happened.

Jill stood over them triumphantly. A sense of rich satisfaction flowed through her.

Tom had a certain look on his face. He began to struggle to his feet.

"Time to be gone," thought Jill. She ran like the wind down the beach.

The boys were after her. She dodged and twisted, and doubled back on her tracks. She was a good runner and very agile, but the boys were also quick on their feet.

It was Bernard who eventually grabbed her. He seemed to be quite lacking in brotherly affection. She kicked violently, but Tom grabbed her ankles. In a moment she was hanging between them like an animated hammock.

"One to be ready," breathed Bernard.

"Two to be steady," added Tom.

"Three to be off," they chanted together. For a moment a squealing Jill was airborne. Then there was a loud splash. The boys shook hands solemnly on the beach.

Suddenly a loud clanging came from the bungalow. Auntie Su was standing at the door, banging something with all her might.

"Dinner time," echoed faintly on the breeze. Hurriedly they climbed the wooden steps, and hastened up the field. The day was so hot that there was no need to get changed. They carried their clothes with them.

Jill slipped her shoes on at the gate, and disappeared inside to change.

The boys went out to their hut, and left a large amount of sand on the floor. They put the swimming trunks out on the hedge to dry.

On the way in to lunch, Bernard showed Tom where the water supply came from. No water main here. A great water tank stood at the rear of the bungalow. Water from the roof ran down into it.

"Do you mean to say we drink it straight from the roof?" demanded Tom. He felt slightly sick.

"The drinking water is boiled first," Bernard explained.

Nevertheless Tom refused a glass of water at lunch time, and then delightedly explained to Jill how the water she had just drunk came from a great tank filled with creepycrawlies.

Uncle Fred had been mending the patch in the chapel ceiling during the morning. He wanted some help in the afternoon to clean up the floor where the plaster had dropped.

"I'll stroll across when the boys have finished drying the dishes for me," Auntie Su offered.

"May I come, too?" asked Jill, eagerly.

* * *

So the boys were left with a chance to get in touch with Mr. Danvers. They had planned to swim out to the *Pied Piper* together, but Moby saved them the trouble.

He beached his dinghy and came up to the post office while they were having lunch and cleaning up. So it was quite easy to bid him a polite "Good afternoon," and accompany him back to the dinghy.

"Can we share a secret with you, sir?" Tom could be very polite when it suited him.

As they walked down the lane, they poured out the story of their night adventure. Much to their relief, Mr. Danvers seemed definitely interested.

"This calls for a Council of War," he said, melodramatically.

He rowed them out to the *Pied Piper* and over chocolate cookies and orangeade, he questioned them carefully.

"This must be a secret," he said firmly. "It is far too good a story to spoil with policemen clumping around."

"I would like to let Jill into it," said Bernard.

"But of course, just the three of you, and myself. Now it seems to me that we must keep a round-the-clock watch on the wreck—or at any rate keep an eye on it as much of each day and each night as we can manage.

"You were up last night, so I will watch tonight. I work late anyhow. I expect you saw me through the porthole last night?"

The boys nodded.

54

"Then you can watch the night after until about 2 A.M. I might row over to the wreck with you then and have a look around myself."

"Why not tonight?" asked Tom, eagerly.

Mr. Danvers smiled.

"There's no holding you, is there? But not tonight. I want you both to be feeling fresh if I keep you up at night. No use having you dropping off to sleep in the middle of a watch, you know! Besides, I would like to have seen something suspicious for myself before we go nosing around."

"Fair enough," Tom admitted.

"Now I must row you ashore. We don't know who might be watching, and we don't want them to get suspicious. Also I have work to do."

"Sorry we interrupted you," said Bernard.

"That's all right, but I think we must have some kind of signal. Let me think. I have to get my work done by a deadline or my publisher will go crazy."

Moby disappeared inside the cabin and re-emerged carrying a triangular flag. It was adorned with a figure of a piper dressed in pied garments of gold and red.

"When I fly my flag, you may come and visit me, if you wish. When no flag is flying you MUST NOT, positively MUST NOT come near the boat."

"What if we have something to report?"

"Then hang your white towel on the hedge up there by your bungalow. I can see it quite clearly from here. All the same, you MUST wait for the flag. When I get an inspiration, I have to get it down on paper while the idea is fresh. I have a fiendish temper if I'm disturbed when I'm writing. You have no idea. No, I'm serious. I

55

don't care if they are stealing the crown jewels, or blowing up St. Paul's Cathedral, if I am in the middle of a chapter I MUST NOT be interrupted. Is that clear?"

"We must remember not to put a towel on the hedge unelss we have news," said Bernard.

"No place for absent-mindedness in this operation," Mr. Danvers agreed.

"Thanks for the orangeade."

He rowed them ashore.

8
Apollyon Crags

"It's the sweetest little chapel!" Jill was bubbling over with enthusiasm. "Kerosene lamps, with brass bowls, hanging from the ceiling. Pews made of wood from a timber ship that was wrecked long ago, and a harmonium, and a hymnboard. Everything is there. Uncle Fred has mended the ceiling, and there wasn't too much mess at all."

"Jill has worked very hard." Auntie Su shot a meaningful look at Tom, who had been about to say something. He colored slightly, and closed his mouth without a comment.

"What else needs to be done, Jill?" asked Bernard.

Jill thought for a moment.

"Well, there's a bulletin board outside. Tom, you're good at art—could you do a poster, do you think?"

"Of course," said Tom, meltingly. "How about HEAR BERNARD! Or perhaps BERNARD'S BACK. No! I've got it. 'St. Bernard barks again.'"

He caught Uncle Fred's eye, and became suddenly serious.

"I'll do the poster, Jill. I promise. No nonsense. I would like to do something to help, really."

"Can I play the harmonium?" Jill begged.

"Of course you can." replied Auntie Su. "Do you think you can play it well enough, though?"

"It isn't very different from the piano really, once you've got used to the stops. I mustn't forget to pedal either—otherwise there won't be any air to work the reeds. Those little boards you push your knees against, they make it go loud or soft. So it's quite easy really."

"Has it got a monkey?"

"Bernard! You know perfectly well that's a barrel organ, not a harmonium."

"Yes, but I was thinking, if Tom put on one of those little red hats with a tassel. . . ."

"Listen, boys," said Auntie Su as seriously as she could, "you must stop making jokes about it all. Otherwise, when Sunday comes, I shall start remembering something you have said and get a fit of the giggles."

"Nothing they have said should make anyone giggle," said Jill primly. "Groan, yes. Giggle, no!"

* * *

Later that evening the boys invited Jill over to the bungalow, and to make amends they told her all that had happened so far. The midnight adventure. Their conversation with Mr. Danvers.

"You're rotten! Rot—tot—tiddley—ot. Rotten!" she said. "Holding out on me all this time!"

"It's the first real chance we've had," pleaded Bernard. "You will keep the secret, won't you?"

"I've a good mind not to!"

"Of course she won't tell!" said Tom, confidently. "Jill's a good sport—even if she is your sister!"

"Mr. Danvers says we are all to have a good sleep tonight, and he'll keep watch. Then the next night we'll all go over to the wreck and explore." Bernard explained.

"How do you know you can trust Mr. Danvers?" asked Jill.

"Of course we can trust him," said Tom, indignantly. "He's a really good sort!"

"Is he?"

"What do you mean, Jill?" asked Bernard. "What reason do you have for not liking him?"

"Oh, nothing. It's just that . . . no, I don't know. Of course he must be all right. You said you saw him through the porthole when the light was on the wreck?"

"Yes."

"Well then, there must be someone else . . . unless. . . ."

"Unless what?"

"Oh, nothing."

Just then they heard a knock at the porch door. It was Uncle Fred. He was wearing a gray turtleneck sweater, and carrying some lengths of rope in his hand.

"Have you discovered Apollyon Crags yet?" he wanted to know.

"No, where are they?" asked Bernard. "It sounds formidable."

"I wondered whether you would like to come with me. I am going there this evening to pick up some driftwood."

"Yes, please," they chorused.

* * *

"Storn is composed of three main hills with valleys between," explained Uncle Fred, as they made their way through the fields.

"Nothing grows on the hilltops. The rock is too near the surface. You could never plow the ground. It is only good for brambles, and rough grass. . . . The valleys are quite different. We grow flowers early in the year, and then potatoes."

The walk was taking them to the northern end of the Island. It was a stiff climb at first, with a more gradual descent into a valley. Then through some fields, and up a stile to get over a fence.

"I've got a cramp," complained Jill.

"Shouldn't eat so much!" Bernard was unsympathetic.

"Listen to who's talking," jeered Tom.

They sat down on an outcrop of rock for a few minutes until Jill got her breath back.

Next came another stiff climb. Then they were on high, uncultivated moorland.

A lark rose from almost at their feet, and soared heavenwards, a flash of white showing in its rapidly fluttering wings. In almost every direction that they looked was the sea.

"It feels as though you are on top of the world," gasped Jill. "I should think if there was a gale we would be blown right off."

At one place the ground ran down sharply at their feet. Beyond stretched the gloomy magnificence of "Wreckers' Bay."

It was an ominous stretch of large rocks. At one end of the bay, the incessant battering of the waves had torn away the undercliff, leaving a dangerous overhang. At the other end of the bay, Apollyon Crags blotted out the skyline.

"Can you see the Devil's face?" asked Uncle Fred.

Tom put his head on one side.

"No," he replied. "No . . . but there's a remarkable resemblance to Bernard!"

The huge crags had withstood the ocean breakers through timeless centuries. To the imaginative, they seemed to take the shape of a twisted and malformed figure, surmounted by a leering, diabolical face. They dominated, like some monstrous idol, the gaping bay which had been littered with the debris of so many wrecks.

"It's awesome!" breathed Jill.

As they scrambled down into the bay, the green earth was springy under their feet. As they got lower down, the view changed. Seen from closer at hand the crags seemed more friendly. The bay itself was magnificent.

It was, in fact, a double bay with a neck of land between. The bay, which looked out towards Corfulwy, was more sheltered. It had been hidden from their view by the outcrop of a hill.

"It's an isthmus," said Bernard, confidently.

"Where are the reindeer?" asked Tom.

"I said 'Isthmus,' not Christmas. An isthmus is a narrow neck of land."

"With a fathead at one end of the neck!" finished Tom, neatly.

"What did I bring you for?" asked Bernard.

"Any wood below high-water mark is ours for the taking," lectured Uncle Fred. "You mustn't touch anything above high-water mark—those piles of wood on the grass belong to neighbors of mine. We bring the wood up and then carry it home at our leisure. Nobody would dream of touching anybody else's."

"Do you have any policemen on the Island?" asked Tom.

"If we did, you would be under arrest by now," said Uncle Fred chuckling.

"One on you that time, Tom!" said Bernard, grinning.

"No need for a policeman," said Uncle Fred. "We all know one another. Nothing can happen on these islands without someone hearing of it."

Tom and Bernard glanced at one another significantly. Jill opened her mouth to say something, and then shut it again, biting her lip.

"I remember when this bay was full of the carcasses of dead cattle," reminisced Uncle Fred. "It was a beastly job hauling them in and burying them."

"Very beastly," agreed Tom.

But Uncle Fred, who was not used to puns, seemed not to have heard him.

"The crags are about two hundred feet high," Uncle Fred went on, "but I have often seen them covered with spray in bad weather."

They returned home by another route. This took them close to the seashore by the channel between Storn and Corfulwy. The water was sheltered, and formed a natural harbor. Several boats were anchored near the shore. None of them compared with *Puffin*. Two of the boats were what Jill called "real boats." The hulls of these were dark blue. Their bulwarks were black. Each carried a registration number painted in large red letters. They were fishermen's boats, designed for work in the worst of weather.

"John and Ernie get their living from the sea," explained Uncle Fred. "Mostly lobster pots. The hotels on Main Island are a good market in the summer."

To reach the path for home, it was necessary to pass through Ernie's front garden. This was full of chickens. Jill wondered what people on the mainland would think if a bunch of strangers came charging through the garden uninvited.

Mrs. Ernie was sitting on her porch, knitting and enjoying the last of the evening sunshine. She did not seem the least surprised to see Uncle Fred, and gave them a cheery wave as they passed. Shutting the gate carefully behind them, they took the winding path which led homewards.

Uncle Fred referred to the path as a "road." This surprised them a little. It was barely wide enough for a horse and cart, and it was covered with gravel from the beach. Occasionally an even narrower path branched off from it to lead to a gray cottage by the sea. They only saw one building which could be fairly described as a house. Even that did not seem very large.

As they turned the last corner, they found themselves in the Main Street. This was the "town" of Storn. It was no more than a small row of cottages nestling against the hillside. One of them had a weatherbeaten notice over the door which declared that it was the post office. By it stood a familiar red booth. This was the Island's only telephone. Tom looked in. As well as the usual box for money, he saw a handle to turn.

"Look, Jill," he said solemnly, "the telephone works by clockwork."

Science was not Jill's favorite subject. She had a strong suspicion that Tom was teasing her. But she said nothing, and contented herself with tossing her head.

"Dad used to have something like that in his office," said Bernard.

"Yes," said Uncle Fred. "When you turn the handle it rings the exchange at Main Island. Then they put you onto a radio link across the water to England . . . that is if Molly Stephens at the exchange has got time to put down her knitting."

It was beginning to get chilly. Dusk was falling. Apart from the post office there were no other shops, although at the other end of the street was an old shack which displayed a window full of oil paintings.

"They are all paintings of the islands," said Uncle Fred. "An artist comes over from the mainland, and stays here for his vacation. I expect he sells enough of those paintings to pay for the trip."

"Not a bad idea," said Tom, thoughtfully. Peering in through the window he could see that the paintings were really very good. He decided he had better wait for a few years before he set up in competition.

The town had an unusual appearance. Uncle Fred's house, and those of his neighbors, had all been built as though they had turned their backs on the main street. If you wanted to get to the post office, you had to go out of the back gate.

"Our front gate is at the back," explained Uncle Fred, succinctly.

"Very clear," said Tom, gravely.

64

There was no garden behind the house. It was all in front. The houses had been built this way so that they would face the sea, and would look away from the hillside. This also meant that they faced due south, and therefore got the full benefit of the sunlight.

The only traffic in the street was animal. Two donkeys stood looking wistfully over Uncle Fred's gate.

"They've got their eye on your lettuce," said Bernard.

There was a pause while Jill patted the donkeys. Evidently they were used to this treatment. They seemed to endure it, rather than welcome it. What did seem to interest them was investigating the contents of the boys' pockets.

"Be my guest," exclaimed Tom. He produced a lemon drop which had been in his pocket for a long while. The donkey didn't seem to mind the hairs and fluff which were stuck to it.

"They are not as affectionate as Prince," said Jill.

"True," Uncle Fred agreed. "Still, they are loyal to one another. Sometimes one of them is harnessed to pull a cart from the beach. When he moves off, the other one strolls along, too, to keep him company!"

They shooed the donkeys away and went through the gate, taking care to shut it behind them.

"Donkeys are all very well," said Uncle Fred, "but they would make short work of my vegetables if they got the chance. No more principles than Tom here!"

"Do you mind!" said Tom, indignantly.

9
Jill Investigates

"Plunk!" Tom had fastened a cardboard target to a piece of driftwood, and leaned it against the chest of drawers. He was now sitting up in bed in his pajamas firing slugs at the target with his air pistol. The morning sunlight was streaming in through the windows.

Bernard, who had washed and dressed, was sitting on his bed reading his Bible.

"I don't see why you have to read the Bible *every* day," objected Tom. "I can understand that religion's all right in its place. But don't you think you're overdoing it a bit?"

"I don't have to read it; I like reading it," said Bernard.

"Come off it!" exclaimed Tom.

Bernard colored slightly.

"Well, to be absolutely honest, I don't always enjoy it," he admitted. "Some parts are more interesting than others. I think it depends on me a little, too. And some days it's easier to pray than other days."

"I prayed once," said Tom casually. He sighted down the barrel, and squeezed the trigger. "Plunk!"

"Did you?"

"Yes." Tom laid the pistol on the bed, and rolled over on one elbow to face Bernard. "I asked God to prove Himself to me, that's if there was a God. Nothing happened though!"

"What did you expect to happen?"

"Oh, I dunno. I suppose it wasn't the right kind of prayer to pray really. . . ."

"I think it was a good prayer," said Bernard. "God might still answer it."

Tom picked up the pistol and pointed it in the direction of Bernard.

"How do you know God exists?" he demanded.

"Is that thing loaded?" asked Bernard.

"No."

"Good. Well, there's evidence that Jesus Christ rose from the dead. If he did, then I would say it was worth listening to what he had to say about God, wouldn't you?"

"Is that the only reason why you're a Christian?"

"Not really. . . . I was converted you see. I asked Jesus to come into my heart . . . and I know he did."

"How do you know?"

"I can't explain it. But Jesus is as real to me as you are."

"Sounds spooky to me," pronounced Tom, judicially. He loaded the pistol again and plunked another slug into the target.

"Tom."

"Yes."

"You could ask Jesus to make you a Christian, too."

There was a silence.

"Look here, Bernard, I would like to be like you.

Honest I would. But don't you see, it's no use saying things just to please you. I've got to know. And I don't see how I can ever know."

"Don't you ever wish your sins were forgiven?"

"I don't think I'm any worse than anybody else. . . . Besides, what about Darwin?"

"The only time I believe in evolution is when I look at you," said Bernard, cheerfully.

* * *

Jill was not sure that she knew how to use the telescope, but she was determined to try.

"Why is it that only Bernard is supposed to be interested in this sort of thing?" she wondered to herself.

She had wakened very early. Her window faced towards the sunrise, and a golden sunbeam slanting across her pillow had aroused her. It was about 5 A.M.

Even Auntie Su would not be awake for another hour at least. So Jill had the world to herself. She would try the telescope while no one was around to disturb her. She could look without Tom making stupid remarks.

She found the huge telescope leaning in a corner of the porch. Its wooden tripod was still outside. Uncle Fred had said that the telescope was used for submarine spotting in the first world war.

"I hope I don't drop it!" Jill gasped to herself. She was glad no one was around.

After one or two false tries, she managed to drop the spike on the telescope into the brass fitting of the tripod. A butterfly screw made it secure.

Jill put her eye to the eye-piece.

"At least I don't have to put any money in it," she

congratulated herself. A circle of blue sky swam hazily into view. "I must be careful not to point it at the sun. It would blind me."

An indistinct blur of green told her that she had found one of the islands.

"How do I focus?" She found the knob and turned it gently. To her delight she could make out the wharf at Main Island. Uncle Fred had told Bernard that you could see a cat walking on the wharf with the aid of that telescope. Either his eyes were better than Jill's or there were no cats!

By a process of trial and error she trained the telescope on the *Puffin*.

"It almost feels as though I could reach out and touch the mast!"

Then a thought struck her. She swung the telescope around in a circle and tried to pick up the wreck. But it was not easy. It was too near to the angle of the sun.

Leaving the telescope for a moment she shaded her eyes and gazed towards the wreck. It looked much as usual.

Between the wreck and the shore a small boat was bobbing up and down. A man in it seemed to be fishing. His build was familiar.

Very carefully Jill adjusted the telescope. It took several moments to pick up the boat at all. She could see nothing but waves at first.

"That's it . . . steady now!" She turned the brass knob a fraction.

"I thought so! It's Mr. Danvers. He must like to go fishing if he gets up at this time in the morning. . . . P'raps he's got nothing for breakfast!"

Suddenly Jill stiffened. She clutched the telescope. "Whatever is he doing?"

To the casual observer Mr. Danvers was evidently fishing. He was almost ostentatiously waving a fishing rod in the air. But Jill's telescope was so powerful that she could observe his every movement. No casual observer from the shore would have noticed the small oblong waterproof packet that he was fastening to the end of his line. There was a splash as the packet hit the water. The line began to run off the reel. It seemed to be a very long line.

Jill was trembling with excitement. The eyepiece misted up. She rubbed it with her handkerchief, and peered again.

"Lost him! No! There he is!" Mr. Danvers was rowing towards the shore. His fishing rod slanted from the stern of the boat. The line trailed behind. It seemed perfectly natural.

"I won't be able to see him once he gets near the rocks," thought Jill.

Mr. Danvers disappeared from view. It was about five minutes before he appeared again. Jill saw through the telescope that the fishing rod no longer had a line attached to it at all.

"He mustn't see me spying on him!" She left the telescope pointing down towards Main Island, and slipped back indoors to her bedroom. From behind the curtains she had a good view of the *Pied Piper*.

Mr. Danvers secured his dinghy, and climbed heavily aboard.

"So that's that!" Her first impulse was to waken the boys.

"No . . . there's no hurry. Moby wouldn't have gone to all that trouble if he was leaving today. I was right after all. I never did trust him."

She sat on the end of the bed and thought and thought. The more she thought the more frightened she became, and yet the more determined.

"I'll show those boys. They held out on me, going off on their own in the middle of the night having adventures. I'll have an adventure."

Silently she slipped out of the house, and taking care to keep out of sight of the *Pied Piper* she made her way up through the fields. As soon as she felt safe she began to run and walk, run and walk, hurrying as fast as she could. She grazed her knee on a stone wall, but she hurried on past low bushes and brambles. She was determined to find where Moby's line came ashore, and itching to know what was at the other end of it. . . .

10
Moby's Plan

"I can't think where Jill has gone." Auntie Su's voice was anxious. "She isn't in her room. Her bed isn't made. It's not like her."

"I expect she's just gone for a stroll," said Uncle Fred, soothingly. "It's a beautiful day."

"Here come the boys. . . . Have you seen Jill?" asked Auntie Su.

"No! Why? Isn't she here? Perhaps she's gone to talk to Prince. . . ."

"Well, we won't wait breakfast for her . . . no doubt she will turn up before long," Auntie Su decided.

Auntie Su had just served eggs and bacon when there was a knock at the door.

"Answer that, will you, Tom," said Uncle Fred. They heard Tom's voice at the door.

"Why, hallo, Mr. Danvers. You're not swimming this morning."

"Do come in, Mr. Danvers," begged Auntie Su. "Would you like some coffee? What about breakfast?"

Mr. Danvers settled himself on a chair.

"No breakfast, thank you. A cup of coffee sounds delightful. I've been out fishing," he volunteered.

"Did you catch anything?" asked Bernard.

"Not a bite! But that's not what I came to ask you about."

"What can we do for you, Mr. Danvers?" asked Uncle Fred.

"Well, I've an idea that might amuse your young visitors. Where is Jill, by the way?"

"We think she's gone out for a walk," replied Tom.

"Ah . . . well she is involved, too. I wondered whether you would like me to set up a treasure hunt?"

"A treasure hunt!" exclaimed Bernard and Tom simultaneously.

"Yes. As a matter of fact I have already hidden a prize. But I haven't put out the clues yet."

"It wouldn't be dangerous, would it?" asked Auntie Su, doubtfully.

"Not a bit of it." Mr. Danvers laughed. "I always remember an uncle of mine who put on a treasure hunt for my brother and me when we were young. I thought I would like to do the same."

"Is there a prize?" asked Tom, practically.

"Tom!" Auntie Su exclaimed reprovingly.

Mr. Danvers did not seem to mind. "Very sensible question. Yes, certainly there is a prize."

Just at this moment Jill arrived.

"You're very late for breakfast, Jill," said Uncle Fred.

"We've eaten it all," said Bernard, grinning. Jill looked white-faced and serious, but before she could say anything the boys began to tell her about the treasure hunt.

A wave of relief flooded over her. This then was the

explanation. What a good thing she had not blurted out her suspicions! Mr. Danvers would have been shocked to think that she had been regarding him as a criminal. But she knew where the treasure was hidden before the hunt began. What could she do about that? She felt a little dizzy.

"Are you all right, Jill?" asked Auntie Su.

She pulled herself together.

"Yes, thank you, Auntie. I think it is a lovely idea. Could you pass the cornflakes, Bernard?"

As he left, Mr. Danvers paused on the porch for a quiet word with Auntie Su.

"Gets a bit lonely sometimes," he said, confidingly. "Wife left me a few years ago. No children, you know. I hope you don't mind?"

Auntie Su nodded sympathetically. She and Fred had always wanted a family.

"So long as they are not a nuisance to you. . . ."

* * *

Presumably inspiration came to Moby when he returned to the *Pied Piper*. No flag flew at the masthead all that morning.

They took a swim, and dived from the deck of *Puffin*. The sound of a typewriter at work came faintly on the breeze.

"I wonder if he saw anything last night?" said Bernard.

"Nothing dramatic. He would have managed to get a message to us somehow," replied Tom. Bernard nodded his head in agreement.

"Where did you disappear to this morning, Jill?" Tom asked suddenly.

Jill colored slightly.

"Oh, nowhere in particular. I just went for a walk."

Time hung rather heavily until lunchtime. Then, just when they had finished clearing away, they saw Moby hoisting his bright little flag. Eagerly they hurried down to the beach, and found him waiting with the dinghy.

On board the *Pied Piper*, after some good-humored joking, they settled down for a planning session.

"First of all, about the treasure hunt," said Mr. Danvers. "I thought it would be fun for you anyhow, but also that it would give us excellent cover for any activities we get involved in while watching the wreck."

"Did you see anything last night?" asked Tom.

"Not a thing."

"Perhaps we imagined it," said Bernard, with a sigh.

"Well, I am not so sure," Moby replied. "I wouldn't have thought that you did." He paused. "Actually, the most likely explanation is that some local fisherman is quietly looting what scrap he can for sale. But you never know . . . it might be something more interesting. Let's hope so."

"When do we begin the treasure hunt?" asked Bernard.

"Well, I had thought originally that it would take place this afternoon. But then, I got a perfectly splendid idea this morning, and that had to come first. So I haven't had time to put the clues around the island yet. Then again, it is a pity to rush it. I expect to be around for a few days yet. Perhaps if you can give me a clear afternoon tomorrow I'll wander around and plant the clues. No stalking me. That wouldn't be fair. Then the next day you could spend the day on solving it, weather

76

permitting. And we might have a celebration feast on board in the evening. How about that?"

"What about watching the wreck?" Tom wanted to know.

"Yes. Can you creep out for an hour or two tonight? I will pick you up from those rocks over there at about midnight, and we'll row across and have a quiet look around. We won't be able to go on board though, far too dangerous."

"I wonder whether there's a monster octopus hiding in the boiler room," said Tom.

"Ooh, Tom, don't. I can't stand octopusses," said Jill.

"Octopi."

"Pusses or pies, I can't stand them," said Jill decidedly.

"So that's your villain, Jill!" chaffed Bernard, as they walked back towards the house, having said good-by to Moby.

"He's rather sweet really," agreed Jill. "Silly of me to be suspicious. Auntie Su thinks that he's lonely. He must be awfully rich and clever . . . but he's not all that happy. Perhaps we are happier than he is!"

Jill hated having secrets. But at the moment she could not bring herself to confide in anyone. She felt foolish, and rather ashamed of herself. Fortunately she had not been able to reach the treasure. Moby had evidently fastened the other end of the fishing line to a cork float at a little distance from the shore. If Jill had not been looking for something of the kind she would never have noticed it. The cork looked like just another bit of flotsam. Only it did not drift away. Presumably it was anchored somehow. She had been tempted to swim out, but had realized that the others would be waiting breakfast for her.

Now what was she to do? She did not want to spoil the treasure hunt for the boys. She did not want Mr. Danvers to know that she had spied on him. She had not meant to be nosy, but she realized that it would seem as though she had been. She could hardly admit that she had thought he was a criminal. In the end, she decided she would confide in Auntie Su, but not yet. . . . She couldn't quite bring herself to talk about it yet.

11
Jill Makes a Discovery

The vigil that night was rather disappointing. Mr. Danvers kept his promise to row them out towards the wreck, but he did not go very far from shore.

There was a swell on the water and instead of taking the risks Tom would have liked, Mr. Danvers behaved disappointingly like any other grown-up with sole responsibility for three young people out late without permission.

Bernard wondered whether perhaps being an author he lived in a world of dreams. Bernard could understand that. He was inclined to do the same himself. He made glorious plans, and then found that cold reality was more difficult to manage. There was no light at all on the wreck. Bernard was rather relieved. Probably if they had seen a light, Mr. Danvers would not have known what to do about it. Perhaps it was just a game to him. He had never really believed that anything criminal was taking place.

In which case, it is really great of him to give us this adventure, thought Bernard.

Tom, who was feeling deflated because Moby had refused to let him handle the oars, was thinking that it was anything but an adventure. That was the worst thing about grown-ups. Mr. Danvers seemed better than most, but even so, he was too cautious. Grown-ups never took enough risks, never had enough imagination.

Tom wished he hadn't brought Mr. Danvers into it. Left to himself, Tom could have stolen a boat and rowed to the wreck himself. Bernard might have been difficult over that. He would probably have had some screwy idea that it would be wrong to take a boat. Oh well, what was the use, he thought. Nothing would happen. Mr. Danvers would see to that.

"I feel sick!" said Jill suddenly.

"You would!"

"I can't help it. . . . I do feel sick."

"It's the way the tide is running," explained Mr. Danvers. "I think we had better be getting back. . . . No sign of life on the wreck."

Jill managed to hold out without disgracing herself. Mr. Danvers put them ashore. They crept silently back to their beds, and were soon sound asleep.

* * *

Jill often wondered later what would have happened if the owl had not wakened her. She was seldom a heavy sleeper, and through staying up late for the expedition she had made herself what her mother called "over-tired."

She felt wretched. She wanted to sleep, yet could not. There were eerie shadows in the room, and she pulled the sheets over her head. She felt wider awake than ever.

She found herself thinking about Moby again, and in

the dark her suspicions began to return. Was it really natural for an author to spend his time arranging a treasure hunt for three youngsters he hardly knew?

She made herself throw back the sheets and get out of bed. She stood at the window gazing out. The *Pied Piper's* lights were on. The boat looked very pretty, with reflections of light on the water. Moby's head and shoulder were visible through a porthole.

Jill mentally gave herself a shake and went back to bed.

"You're just being silly," she told herself. The bed was not the least bit comfortable. She felt "itchy" and hot. The pillow seemed full of lumps. She turned it over, and gave it a thump.

"Would any intelligent grown-up hide the prize for a treasure hunt in several fathoms of water, and out of reach of the shore?" she asked herself. "Surely he would think that Tom would be bound to drown himself trying to get to it."

She got out of bed and sat with her head in her hands trying to think. She felt so muddled, but she must make herself think clearly.

"Why should Moby lie?" she wondered. "He didn't know that I found the treasure. He couldn't have seen me."

Suddenly the palms of her hands felt clammy and her throat was dry.

"Could he have seen me? Suppose he was having his morning swim. . . . If he was hiding something, then he would almost certainly swim back towards it, to make sure the coast was clear. . . .

"He *did* see me!" she gasped it aloud.

Then a terrible thought struck her. Suppose he was on his way up to the house to silence her forever!

She rushed to the window. The silhouette was still at the porthole.

For a moment she felt comforted. Then a hideous suspicion dawned in her mind.

"WHY HASN'T HE MOVED?"

The door creaked faintly as she opened it. Holding her breath she tiptoed through the empty hall. Uncle Fred did not usually bother to lock the door. There were no criminals on the islands.

"And no policemen, either!" thought Jill, with a shudder.

Tremblingly she fitted the telescope into its tripod. The brass was cold to her touch. Terrified though she was, she was longing to convince herself that it was all imagination.

The porthole came into focus. Moby's head and shoulders were a blur. She turned the knob very slightly. Her hands were shaking. Her teeth chattered with the cold.

Then she stifled a shriek and whimpered instead. The figure at the porthole was all too obviously one of those heads of polystyrene which people use to keep wigs in shape. A beret was on top of it, and a jacket thrown about it. Convincing enough at a distance, the telescope revealed every flaw.

Moby was not on the *Pied Piper*. He might be anywhere! He might be coming to get her! A twig snapped down by the gate of the field. She realized that she was clearly visible in the moonlight. Silently she sped back into the house, and into her room. She checked the bolt on the window, pulled the curtains across, put a chair under the door handle, and leaped under the blankets.

"Dear Lord Jesus," she prayed, frantically, "do please take care of me. I'm so frightened. . . ."

She did not waken until Auntie Su banged the breakfast gong . . . .

As she hurriedly dressed herself, Jill turned over in her mind whether or not to blurt out all her suspicions. Things always seem different in the daylight, and she was feeling a little ashamed of her fright the night before.

The only real fact she had to go on was that Moby had put a dummy of himself at a porthole. She was sure she had seen that, but could she convince Uncle Fred and Auntie Su? They would almost certainly confront Moby with her suspicions. He would no doubt be able to lie his way out smoothly enough. He might easily say that Jill had imagined it. It would be his word against hers.

She would tell the boys, of course. Even they might be a little hard to convince. They had never shared her suspicions of Mr. Danvers.

Jill was late for breakfast. The boys were already seated at the table, and the joking began right away. Tom in particular was most insulting. Jill, who had had a bad night, felt he was being silly.

"Just like Jill," he jeered. "No stamina."

"The Youth Club went on a hike last year. Jill wore stupid shoes, and before we had gone a mile she was moaning about her feet."

"What has that got to do with being late for breakfast?" snapped Jill.

"Nothing at all! Nothing at all! It's just that I really feel quite sorry for people who sleep in, don't you, Bernard?"

"Especially the fat ones," teased Bernard, adding fuel to the flames. Jill was not really fat, but Bernard knew that she was touchy on the subject of overeating.

"Fat, sleepy ones. . . ." agreed Tom.

Jill was so exasperated that she stuck out her tongue at him.

"That's enough, boys," said Auntie Su, sternly. "A joke is one thing, but you are overdoing it."

"And she is overdoing the butter on that toast," whispered Bernard to Tom.

"Bernard!"

"Sorry, Uncle Fred."

Jill continued her breakfast in stony silence. Silly, stupid boys. She would show them. They knew they were two to one. Just like when they threw her in the water the other day. It wasn't fair. Bernard ought to take her side. He was her brother. She would show him. She would show them all.

"Are you coming down to the beach?" asked Bernard when breakfast was over. Jill knew that he was trying to make up to her, but she was still angry.

She tossed her head. "No, thank you. I shall go for a walk on my own."

"We'll come too, if you like," offered Tom.

"I prefer to be alone," replied Jill coldly. "I can't bear the company of juveniles."

She turned on her heel and made her exit. She was glad she had thought of saying "juveniles." She felt she had scored one there.

"What's bitten her?" Tom wanted to know.

"Well, we did lay it on pretty strong," admitted Bernard.

"Shall we go after her?"

"No, better let her cool off first. She'll get over it."

"Tell you what," said Tom, brightening. "We'll go to the post office and buy her a candy bar . . . a sort of peace offering."

"Good idea, then we can help her eat it!"

"Pig."

"Listen to who's talking!"

12
Jill in Danger

Hurriedly Jill climbed into her swimsuit. Over the top she put a turtleneck blouse, a bright red one which she rather liked. She chose her favorite skirt in preference to jeans. She wanted to feel as grown-up as possible.

She went into the kitchen.

Auntie Su looked up and smiled.

"You do look pretty, Jill," she said, fondly.

"I thought I would just go for a little walk along the cliffs, Auntie." Jill's blue eyes were as innocent as a baby's.

"Lunch is at 12:30. Don't be late, will you."

"Oh no, Auntie. I was so tired this morning."

"It's the sea air. You're not used to it. It will do you a lot of good. Yes, do go for a walk. It will put color in your cheeks."

Jill looked at her reflection in the hall mirror.

"You do look pretty, Jill," she whispered to herself. Then she screwed up her face and went cross-eyed.

"Pretty! Ugh!"

The sea was calm, with hardly any breeze. The waves lapped gently against the base of Apollyon Crags. Sea gulls circled screaming as Jill clambered down towards the bay. The distant horizon was not as clear as usual. It looked as though a mist might be coming, but not for a few hours yet, thought Jill.

She felt very much alone. Apollyon Crags dwarfed her.

She wondered whether they had changed in a thousand years. They would still be there in another thousand years' time, unless the world came to an end. She wondered whether Jesus would come back soon, as her minister had said that he might.

She sat on a small rock as though surveying the veiw. Actually, however, she was keeping a careful lookout for Moby. He must not catch her in this lonely spot. She would never have come without the others if they had not annoyed her so much. She was already regretting her anger. Still, she would show them.

She slipped behind a rock and left her blouse, skirt, and sandals there. The water on the opposite side of the isthmus to Wreckers' Bay was calm and still, but it looked so deep and dark that Jill shivered in the sunlight.

The innocent looking cork was still afloat several yards from the shore.

"Do it now!" Jill told herself, firmly.

She looked down into the depths.

"Nonsense! There are no such things as giant squids."

Holding her nose she jumped from the bank into the water. Her feet did not touch the bottom. Coming to the surface she struck out towards the cork float. Within a few minutes she was climbing triumphantly onto the bank again with the float in her hand. She lay flat on the springy grass for a moment or two looking like a wet seal, and getting her breath back. Then she began to haul on the lines attached to the float. One was plainly an anchor line to prevent the float drifting too far. It was so heavy to pull in that Jill decided to pull the other line in first. She picked up a small piece of driftwood and began to wind the string around it. It was like hauling in a kite, except that the string went down into the water instead of up into the sky.

"Will the string never end?" she asked herself.

She had a large ball of twine on the stick before the package came into sight. Eagerly she pulled in the last few yards.

She disentangled a few streamers of seaweed from the string, and took hold of the parcel. It was securely wrapped. Jill was in a quandary. She was longing to open it, but the string had knotted tightly while the packet was submerged. She knew that she would never be able to retie the knots even if she could get them undone. That in itself seemed unlikely.

"If only I had thought to bring a jackknife or scissors," she said. She could not break the twine, which was strong fishing line.

"At least I can take the parcel home," she thought. Then in the privacy of her room she could unwrap it with care, and if necessary rewrap it without giving herself away.

By holding a length of the twine and rubbing it against a piece of jagged rock with a sawing motion she managed to free the parcel. She then threw the float back into the sea. She tied a stone where the parcel had been, and whirling it around her head sent it plummeting out into the water. Within a few moments the line had disappeared.

By this time her skin had dried, although her suit was still damp. She dressed again, and set out towards home. But how could she conceal the package? She stooped and picked up a handful of short lengths of driftwood. It wasn't much of a disguise, but it was all she could think of. She tucked the package in between the strips of wood.

She began to climb the cliff path that led towards Mrs. Ernie's house. She hurried as fast as she could, and panted with the effort. At the top of the climb the path became a narrow gap between two boulders.

"Going somewhere?"

Moby, his face inscrutable, was blocking her advance. He stood on higher ground, and seemed to tower above her.

Involuntarily Jill gasped.

Moby seized her arm, and the wood clattered to the ground. Moby stooped to pick up the package, and Jill tore her arm free.

She set off frantically running across the high moorland. She glanced behind her, Moby was only a few yards behind, and gaining rapidly. She doubled back in her tracks, and he fell heavily in trying to turn. In a moment, however, he was on his feet. He was a heavy man, but the chase was unequal. She screamed for help, but her voice seemed small in the empty air. Just another cry like those of the sea gulls above.

She doubled back once again, and as she did so twisted her ankle. Moby stood over her panting heavily.

"Are you all right?"

"I think so." Jill got to her feet, and tried standing on the leg.

"Nothing broken." Moby himself was glancing around to make sure no one was in sight.

"Are you going to murder me?" asked Jill in a small voice.

"I never murder people before lunch," said Mr. Danvers. "It spoils my appetite! However, you are quite definitely my prisoner. I have a dinghy just below the cliff edge down here. If your ankle is better, perhaps you would oblige me by getting into it."

"Suppose I refuse?"

"Don't be difficult, Jill. There is nobody within a mile of us. I am not a bully, but I cannot afford to waste time. You and your friends have made things very difficult for me. If I have to knock you out, I will, so just be a good girl and come along quietly."

Discretion seemed the better part of valor. Jill climbed down to the beach with Moby close behind her. Drawn up into the shadows of a small cave was a large black inflatable rubber dinghy. It had a powerful-looking outboard motor. This had been painted a dull black.

"Stand in the cave while I launch this," Moby ordered, simply, and within a few moments he had the dinghy afloat.

"Now listen carefully," ordered Moby. "You are to come straight out of the cave and lie down in the bottom of the dinghy. I shall cover you with these sacks. I don't think anyone is likely to see you, but I don't believe in taking chances."

Jill lay down flat in the boat as she was told. The sacking was coarse, but dry. She heard the engine splutter into life, and the rush of water beneath her.

"You can come out now," Moby called above the noise of the engine.

Jill sat up, putting aside the sacks. They were already way out to sea beyond the wreck; the outboard was very fast. Moby was circling towards the westward rocks. He sped out beyond them. Jill knew that nobody on Storn could possibly see them.

Very soon it became evident that Moby was heading for one of the outlying uninhabited islands. Sea gulls rose and whirled angrily as he eased the boat ashore on the seaward side of the island.

"Jump ashore," commanded Moby.

Jill leaped for the beach and stood waiting for him. She had thoughts of picking up a heavy rock to defend herself, but decided that it was hopeless. Moby secured the dinghy and then paused to light a cigarette.

Jill, who was an imaginative girl, realized that she was now in greater danger than ever. If Moby was dangerous she had no chance of escape. Nobody could see or hear, nobody would know where she had gone. She felt like crying, but instead she tilted her chin defiantly as he came towards her. . . .

13

Marooned

"Wow! I wish he would let me try that," exclaimed Tom, with a whistle of admiration.

It was about eleven o'clock, and the boys, having bought Jill's candy bar, and also eaten some of their own, were sitting down on the beach beside Uncle Fred's skiff.

Tom pointed out towards the *Pied Piper*. Moby, dressed in complete underwater swimming gear, was climbing heavily on board.

"I suppose he has been getting local color for his book," said Bernard.

"Or catching lobsters," added Tom.

A quarter of an hour later, Moby, dressed in an open-necked shirt and gray trousers, clambered into the dinghy of the *Pied Piper* and came rowing slowly towards them. As he sauntered up the beach, Bernard and Tom ran down to meet him.

"Would you mind taking a message to your aunt and uncle?" Moby asked.

"Of course; what is it?"

"Would you tell her that Jill will be late for lunch? You see, I've commandeered her services. It suddenly

93

occurred to me that I promised you a celebration dinner, and I've only got ordinary food on board."

"Scrumptious!" exclaimed Tom.

"So I've put Jill ashore on Corfulwy and asked her to do my week's shopping for me. You know what these village stores are like, and I have given her a list as long as my arm."

"We thought you had been underwater swimming all morning," said Bernard.

"Oh no," replied Moby, easily. "I was just trying out some new gear. I rowed Jill over to Corfulwy before you came down to the beach."

"Auntie doesn't like people being late for lunch," said Bernard.

"But I am sure you can put the blame on me," said Moby, apologetically. "If you scoot up to the house now, you can catch her before she really starts the cooking."

Moby began to turn away. "Tell her not to expect Jill back before about three. I told Jill to buy herself something to eat while she's on Corfulwy, so she won't starve. Oh! And give me a clear afternoon, will you? I want to plant those clues," he called over his shoulder as he strode off down the beach.

Bernard and Tom delivered the message.

"How very odd!" said Auntie Su, banging down a saucepan indignantly. "That man!" she added. "No wonder his poor wife left him."

"He's not as bad as all that, Auntie," pleaded Bernard.

"No, I suppose not. But it's thoughtless all the same. Jill ought to have her meals regularly. A sandwich on

Corfulwy is not like one of my roasts. She won't be back until late. That shop is way over on the other side . . . and the poor mite with a load of shopping. Oh well, it can't be helped, I suppose. But I'm not surprised he sent you with the message. If he had come himself I would have given him a piece of my mind!"

"What's the trouble?" asked Uncle Fred, putting his head around the door. "Were you thinking of making coffee?" he hinted.

"Coffee indeed!" snorted Auntie Su. "That man has sent Jill to Corfulwy to shop for him!"

"Has he though?" said Uncle Fred, looking a little anxious. "That's a pity . . . because I think there is a sea mist coming up. Oh well, they're very neighborly over there. Mrs. Blythe at the stores will see that she comes to no harm."

Just at that moment the air was filled with a deep droning noise. Three times it boomed out.

"That's the Flat Island foghorn," explained Uncle Fred. "There's a lighthouse on Flat Island. When the mist comes up they sound the foghorn. We shall get that noise now until the fog lifts."

"Isn't it a dismal sound?" said Auntie Su. "Sometimes in the winter it goes on for days and nights at a time."

"I think it drove Mrs. Arbutt to her death," said Uncle Fred. "A few winters ago when that thing was blasting away poor Mrs. Arbutt walked out into the water and drowned herself."

"Does her ghost walk?" asked Tom, hopefully.

"Tom!"

"Sorry! I didn't realize she was your friend, of course.

95

Let's go and read books until lunch time, Bernard."

The boys made a hurried exit.

The mist was thin and white sweeping in from the open sea in a faint drizzle of moisture. Familiar landmarks were fast beginning to disappear.

"Bang goes the treasure hunt," said Bernard, sadly. "He'll never be able to put out clues in this weather."

"Poor old Jill on Corfulwy," said Tom.

"It's just as well Moby gave her money for food. . . . At least she won't starve. I expect she is sitting in a cafe eating hot soup at this very moment."

In which case he was quite mistaken.

* * *

When Moby had come up from the shore to where Jill was standing, he sat down on a rock beside her, smoking his cigarette.

"You know," he said sadly, "you and your brother and Tom have been an absolute menace to me all the way through."

"What do you mean?" asked Jill.

Moby flicked the ash from the tip of his cigarette. "I might as well tell you the whole story," he said. "I'm not an author, of course. You've guessed that?"

Jill nodded.

"I've been a lot of things in my time," he went on reminiscently, "but never an author. I was in the navy at one time. I enjoyed that. But it was a long while ago. I might have been an actor, but it seemed like hard work. I don't like hard work, Jill. It bores me. I've a talent for making people believe what I tell them. That makes life easy provided you don't get caught. People lend you money. Then you change your name and disappear."

"I think that's mean!" Jill interrupted him hotly.

"Do you?" Moby sounded indifferent. "Well, I'm a thief, too. Oh, I didn't steal the *Pied Piper*. I paid for her with good hard cash. But I did a few jobs here and there to get the money for her. I've always liked boats since I was in the navy."

He fished the package out of his pocket and weighed it in his hand reflectively.

"The biggest job I ever pulled off was in Italy. I wish I had time to show you the necklace that is in this package. It's really lovely, believe me. The earrings and bracelets are elsewhere, a perfect matching set. You should have seen the mansion in Italy where they came from. I've never seen anything like it, not even in the movies. Once I had done the job, Italy was too hot for me, so I joined a merchant ship, that one that's wrecked over by Corfulwy. It was easy for me to be a sailor. I told you I had been in the navy. I hid the jewels in my cabin, half in a ventilator and half behind an inspection panel. I thought that was being careful, but I never bargained on being wrecked. Who would have thought of that? We had all the navigational equipment, but Neptune still has his moments.

"When we hit the rock it was every man for himself. There were my packets all neatly hidden in the cabin, and the boat was sinking and the lifeboat was leaving. I tell you I was scared that night." He puffed on the cigarette reflectively. "From then on I was determined to get back one day. I thought the ship might have broken up during the winter, but she's stuck fast.

"My cabin is half under water, even at low tide. When the tide is high you can't get near it. It's been

97

very difficult, I tell you. Have you ever tried unscrewing screws that have gone rusty under three feet of water, and not being able to flash a light about more than you can help? Tricky, I tell you. Very tricky. Of course the frogman's kit helps a lot but I've had some nasty moments. I got this package first. It took me all last night to reach the other one. Then I couldn't quite make it. I shall get it this afternoon, though.

"Then you three kids turned up. I had bargained on it being a lonely spot. But of course you had to be here on vacation. And then you had to see me hiding this package. Silly, isn't it! I would have done better to keep it on board, but I never like to have incriminating evidence about. I still don't understand how you managed to spot me."

"Telescope," said Jill simply. "It's very powerful."

Moby slapped his leg. "So that's it. It must be powerful."

He stubbed out his cigarette on a rock. "Well, that's my story. I hoped to fob you off with a treasure hunt. I thought you would swallow that. The boys did, didn't they? But then this morning I saw you were up to something after all. However, there's no real harm done. I was nearly finished here anyway. All I need is an hour or two to make the trip from here to England. Then I change my clothes and disappear. I've never been in prison, so I've no record. No fingerprints. You would be surprised how many criminals are never caught, Jill."

"God will judge them," said Jill, firmly.

"Ah yes, but then you see I don't believe in God. You'll be all right here. Once I get to England I'll phone the customs people and tell them where I've marooned you. I dare say you'll get a helicopter rescue! Whatever you do, don't try and swim for it. There's a perfectly dreadful current around these rocks. You know what Apollyon Crags look like, and Wreckers Bay. Nothing could live in those waters. So stay here. It will only be for a few hours, I promise you."

He strode back to the dinghy. The engine roared. Jill was left alone.

14
Moby Slips Away

"It sounds like a cow with indigestion!" Tom was referring to the foghorn which was disturbing their enjoyment of lunch.

"Just think of the ships at sea, Tom," said Auntie Su. "Men's lives depend upon that noise."

"This fog makes life rather dull," complained Bernard. "How long do you think it will last?"

"It may lift as suddenly as it came," replied Uncle Fred.

"What are you going to do this afternoon?" Auntie Su wanted to know.

"Do you have any poster paints?" asked Tom. "I was thinking I might as well do that poster for the chapel this afternoon. It will be something to do till the fog lifts."

"I have some paper you can use," said Uncle Fred, "but no paints, I'm afraid."

"Tell you what," said Bernard. "Why don't we phone Jill and ask her to bring some paints back from Corfulwy with her. Tom can work out how the letters will fit on the paper, and then when Jill gets back with the paints all he will have to do is to color them in."

"That's a very good idea." Auntie Su seemed relieved. "You see, Uncle Fred and I were thinking that we ought to slip down and visit Mrs. Darrant this afternoon. She's on her own since her husband died last winter, and it's very miserable in these fogs. Will you two be able to keep out of mischief while we are away?"

"Of course, Auntie. While Tom is doing the poster I will try and think of something to say. Sunday is getting uncomfortably near now."

Tom and Bernard got some money and went up to the phone booth. The mist swirled around them. They were glad to shut the door. Tom had been itching to use the strange telephone ever since they had first seen it.

Within a few minutes they were connected with Mrs. Blythe of the main store on Corfulwy.

"Could you please give a message to the young lady if she is still with you?"

"What young lady?" The voice on the other end of the telephone sounded mystified.

"My friend's sister, Jill. She came over to your store to do some shopping this morning. We thought she would probably stay with you till the fog lifted."

"We haven't had any strangers in the store at all this morning," said the voice.

"Oh dear," said Tom, "what can have happened to her. She was rowed across to Corfulwy this morning, and we were quite sure that she would still be with you. Nobody could cross the water in this fog."

"Yes, it is thick," agreed the voice. "Hold the line a minute, will you?"

Tom could hear a conversation going on at the other

end of the telephone. Then Mrs. Blythe returned to the phone.

"Are you still there?"

"Yes."

"Well, listen, my husband has been down at the wharf all morning putting a new plank in the dinghy. He says he is absolutely sure no young lady came ashore this morning. He was down there from eight o'clock until he saw the fog beginning to come up. He's quite certain nobody has landed. You must have made a mistake."

"Yes, I suppose we have," agreed Tom, thoughtfully. "Thank you very much. Sorry to have troubled you."

"That's all right. I hope nothing is wrong."

"Sorry to have troubled you," said Tom, absently, and replaced the receiver.

"What is it?" Bernard's anxiety had been mounting all the way through the conversation.

"Moby is a liar," said Tom. "And if he is a liar, then he may be a crook."

"What do you mean?"

"He never put Jill ashore on Corfulwy this morning. He just told us that to stop us wondering where she was. Jill never trusted him. I reckon he's holding her captive on board the *Pied Piper*."

"What are we going to do?" Bernard was almost wringing his hands. "Tom, we must tell the grown-ups now!"

"Yes, of course we must. But Uncle Fred and Auntie Su have gone out. Look, Bernard, you find them. You had better raise the alarm at the post office, too. I'm going straight down to the beach. I can row out to the *Pied Piper*."

"Tom, you can't. You'll lose your way in the fog and probably capsize yourself."

"I shall do nothing of the kind. In any case, we have got to try it. Anything might be happening to Jill."

"What can you do against Moby? He's strong. Let me come, too!"

"Can't you see, we must have reinforcements, Bernard, and we can't afford to wait. I'll take the air gun. It won't kill him, but it might slow him down."

Bernard would have liked to argue, but Tom was already vaulting over the wall into the garden.

"Do be careful," he called, but the mist had already swallowed Tom up.

Bernard ran up the steps into the post office. A lady, who looked at least ninety years old, was knitting behind the counter.

"Please, I'm in terrible trouble," gasped Bernard.

"Eh?" said the old lady. "You'll find all the candy in that case over there. Just take your pick, my dear. What a terrible fog this is!"

Bernard groaned to himself. There were no police within three miles. Uncle Fred and Auntie Su were halfway across the island visiting a friend. Tom was probably drowning in the channel. Jill was gone. . . . He could see that getting help was going to take some time.

He opened the little door in the counter and bending over put his lips close to the old lady's ear and began to shout. . . .

* * *

104

Tom had grabbed up his air gun, and also a small pocket compass he had been given for Christmas. Tom did not know much about the sea, but he had been out on the moors with his parents. He took the lane to the beach rather than down through the fields. Visibility was poor, but he was able to run at a steady trot. He found Uncle Fred's skiff, dragged it to the water, and leaped aboard.

He found himself rowing in a white circle of mist. The compass was a little help, and would have helped even more if Tom had been more expert with it. However, most of his attention was occupied in handling the oars. The foghorn about which he had complained was his chief guide now. He had a good sense of direction, and he knew where Flat Island was in relation to Storn and Corfulwy.

"If only I knew what the tide was doing," he said as the oars dipped into the water. Unexpectedly he found himself praying, and praying urgently.

A boat loomed suddenly out of the mist. He recognized the *Puffin*. Her anchor chain seemed fairly limp and he surmised from this that the tide could not be running very fast. Perhaps the tide was about to turn? He wished he knew.

"Anyhow, I ought to be able to get my bearings from here," he thought.

In actual fact, of course, his chances were far more remote than he realized. Tom was an eternal optimist. Further out the current began to catch him. He did not worry about this because, surrounded by the mist, he had no idea that his skiff was in the grip of the current. No idea, that is, until the current swept him across the stern of the *Pied Piper* with a thump which sent him sprawling in the bottom of the skiff. One oar slipped from the oarlock and disappeared, floating away into the mist.

If Moby had been on board, Tom would not have had a chance. But the bump did not seem to have disturbed anyone. Tom clambered aboard, and turned to take hold of the rope to secure the skiff to the *Pied Piper*. He made a frenzied grab, but the tail end of the rope was just slipping off the deck. He missed it. He leaned over the side. The skiff was beyond his reach.

"Crumbs!"

He must find Jill. That was more important than the skiff. He hurried into the cabin. There was no typewriter in sight, but on the table was a small portable tape recorder. He switched it on, and the noise of typing filled the air. He switched it off. Stark terror seized him. He had still been uncertain that Moby was a crook. Here was evidence. He was convinced now.

"Jill!" he called anxiously, casting discretion to the winds. There was no reply. A small mahogany door separated the two cabins. He opened it and stepped into the forward cabin. On one side was a bunk bed. On the other, a net shelf with a lifejacket on it, a first aid box, and some emergency flares.

The boat suddenly gave a lurch. Someone was coming aboard. Tom pulled the mahogany door shut, and kneeled, peering through the keyhole. The loaded air gun was in his hand, but he knew that it would not give him much real protection if he was discovered. "At least," he thought, "the skiff won't give me away. It must have drifted nearly to Flat Island by now."

Moby shed his breathing apparatus in the cockpit, and came flapping into the aft cabin, still wearing his rubber suit and frogman's flippers. The navy had taught him all he needed to know about underwater swimming many years before. Indeed, the mist had provided him with ideal cover.

He moved about the cabin, carefully stowing away the tape recorder and other small moveable items. Then he eagerly began to undo two small packages.

"At last!" Tom heard him murmur to himself. It was difficult to see, squinting through the keyhole, but for one moment Tom caught the gleam and flash of jewels.

Moby stood poised irresolutely for one moment, then diving under a seat he produced a cash box into which he dropped the jewels with a rattle. He returned the box to its hiding place.

"And now for some blind navigation," he said to himself. He slipped off his flippers, and went out barefooted into the cockpit. He shut the door behind him, and Tom heard the cough and splutter of the *Pied Piper*'s auxiliary engine. Moby's feet pattered on the deck over Tom's head. The anchor chain rattled over the roller. Moby dropped down into the cockpit with a heavy thump. The *Pied Piper* began to glide forward into the mist.

Tom did not know much about navigation, but he did know that for the next few minutes at least Moby would have his eyes glued to the compass in the cockpit. He would not be able to take his eye from the compass for a moment or disaster was certain.

Tom slipped into the aft cabin and knelt by the seat. It was the work of a moment to open the cash box. The dull glow of the jewels would have thrilled Jill, but Tom had a prosaic mind. He stuffed the contents of the box into his pocket. Then a thought struck him. He had a box of air gun slugs in his pocket. Made of lead, they weighed about the same as the jewels. There was not much risk of him being heard above the noise of the engine, but he was cautious as he tipped the slugs into the box. At least it would rattle when it was picked up. He stuffed the key down a crack in the floorboards. He hoped Moby might think that it had fallen out with the jolting of the boat. Anything to cause delay and confusion! He had not the slightest idea of how he would get out of the situation, but at least he would make things as difficult for Moby as he could.

"Author, my foot," he thought to himself. "Murderer, more like it!"

Then he remembered Jill again, and broke into a cold sweat. He crept back into the forward cabin and closed the door.

15
Disaster

"I'm not half as afraid as I thought I would be," Jill said to herself.

At home the slightest creak of a floorboard would send her head under the bedclothes. Imagination conjured up burglars inside every closet. But now, faced with a real adventure, she was surprised to find that she was almost enjoying it.

The moment Moby had disappeared from sight she started collecting driftwood. By the time the mist came down she already had sufficient for a large bonfire.

"Serves Moby right for being such a heavy smoker!" she said to herself with satisfaction. When she had been forced to lie down in the bottom of the rubber dinghy, she had discovered wedged against the side of the boat one of those cardboard books of matches which are sometimes given away free at restaurants and clubs. Most of the matches had been torn out, but three were left. The book must have fallen from Moby's pocket on some occasion when he was using the dinghy. Jill had not thought it necessary to return the matches.

"Now, my girl, you've got to be very, very careful," she told herself.

There were only three matches. She had heard of primitive savages making a fire by using a bow, and a peg of wood spinning in a hole. It sounded all right in theory, but she suspected that it was one of those cases where the average primitive savage was a great deal smarter at starting a fire than she would be.

There was a hoop of iron on one of the pieces of driftwood. She supposed that with so many granite rocks around she would be able to make some sparks with that—but it might take ages.

"More haste, less speed," she thought to herself. She wondered whether to delay lighting her fire until the fog lifted. But the supply of driftwood seemed inexhaustible. She decided there was no reason to wait. She arranged some of the stones to make a neat fireplace, and laid her fire with great care. She had plenty of dry grass to make a start with, and the driftwood at high tide mark was as dry as a bone.

"Steady now, girl." The first match fizzled and flared and sputtered out. Only two left. Jill drew a deep breath and tried again.

This time there was no mishap. The flame danced in the dry grass. Jill hovered over it attentively. She coaxed it with tiny slivers of wood.

Soon she was able to add larger pieces. The strong yellow flames curled hungrily around them. The blue smoke mingled with the mist. Soon the bonfire had a blazing red hot center, and it was safe to add some real planks.

Jill watched the flames blacken the edges of a large plank. The edges began to turn to black charcoal where the greedy flames took hold of it.

110

"I have enough wood to last for hours," she thought, contentedly. The heat was terrific. Although the mist was behind her, the warmth of the blaze prevented her from feeling cold.

In the distance she heard the "mooing" sound of the Flat Island foghorn.

* * *

Moby's eyes were glued to the compass. He was used to taking risks, but he knew that he was gambling with the safety of the *Pied Piper*. He had never intended to leave the islands with such haste. Now he could not afford to delay. Jill's discovery had upset his plans. While the fog lasted, he was safe from discovery. But once it lifted he might only have a few hours before the police were on his trail. The *Pied Piper* would have to go, of course. Once he was on the mainland he could alter his appearance a little and lie low until the hunt cooled off. He had intended to sell the yacht. Instead he would have to scuttle her.

"Perhaps I can make them think I drowned. . . ." His ingenious mind toyed with alternative ways to escape. But his attention never relaxed as he eased the craft on through the mist. Flat Island foghorn blared close at hand.

"I wish I could have collected the dinghy," he thought to himself. "That outboard would bring a few hundred."

He decided that it was too risky, but he was not unduly upset. He knew the value of the jewels he had recovered. In comparison to those jewels the value of the *Pied Piper* and of the dinghy was chicken feed. He would sail the yacht to the mainland, run her ashore on the rocks, and escape in his frogman's suit.

There was one factor Moby had overlooked. Uncle Fred could have warned him of it. At certain periods of the year there are exceptionally low tides. At that very moment anyone with waders could have walked between Storn and Corfulwy if he knew where the causeway lay.

It was only on such occasions of very low tide that Grinders' rock, with its triple fangs, became a menace to shallow draft boats.

The mist was beginning to lift. The afternoon sun appeared as an indistinct white disk. Moby glanced up and as he did so caught sight of the large fang of Grinders' rock. He swung the helm hard over. The *Pied Piper* began to turn to port, away from the large fang, but as she did so the third and smallest fang ripped through the planking beneath his feet.

Tom was thrown off his feet by the jarring impact. The *Pied Piper* gave a sickening lurch. Something told him that the yacht had received her death wound.

Tom longed to call out for help, but he dared not do so. The floor beneath his feet took on a slant. In the cockpit, Moby was struggling into his breathing apparatus. He came bursting into the cabin. In the stress of the moment he was talking to himself.

"Not again!" Tom heard him say. "Oh, no, not again."

Moby snatched the cash box from its hiding place and groped for the key. When he could not find it, he took the box just as it was.

"If I can get to the rubber dinghy, I can still get away," he said. The *Pied Piper* lurched and settled

112

further into the waves. Moby, with his flippers on his feet, turned on the breathing apparatus. Tom heard the strange tinny, echoing sigh of the equipment. The next moment there was a huge splash, and Moby was gone.

Tom flung open the mahogany door to make his own try for safety. As he did so the *Pied Piper* lurched again. The door into the cockpit had disappeared beneath green water. Tom retreated before the advancing water into the cabin where he had hidden before. He thought his last hour had come. He could not smash through the timbers above his head. He doubted his capacity to swim out through the cockpit. He was caught like a rat in a trap!

He waited for the next lurch to come. But nothing happened. He took a breath and began to think carefully. Was there anything in the cabin he could use to smash a hole with and escape? Nothing seemed to offer itself as a tool. He knew how strong the timbers of an ocean-going yacht would be. Even if he made a hole it might let water in before it let him out!

Desperately he prayed, and as he did so he found himself with a tune in his mind which he had heard Bernard singing on occasion.

"We have an anchor
    that keeps the soul,
    steadfast and sure
    whilst the billows roll. . . ."

"That's it," he cried, excitedly, "an anchor. The *Pied Piper* must have an anchor." He turned to the wall behind him, which was now at an acute angle since the

113

floor sloped so much. He tapped it. It wasn't wooden like the curving sides of the vessel. It was an asbestos panel. He smashed his shoulder against it, and it split. A tangle of ropes, tin cans, and the anchor itself all came slithering out of the forward compartment into the cabin. Tom now had access to the forward hatch. He pushed it up and saw blue sky above his head. The mist was already blowing away. Tom dived back into the cabin and helped himself to the distress flares. Then he squeezed up through the hatchway and sat himself on the bow of the *Pied Piper*.

"I always did enjoy fireworks," he said, chuckling to himself as he watched his distress signal flare. "Oh, and thank You, God," he added.

16
Sunday 6:30

By the time Bernard had succeeded in mobilizing the island, the mist had lifted. Uncle Fred came back from telephoning the police, his face strained and anxious.

"They're sending a helicopter," he said, "but until it arrives it's up to us."

"Tom's safe at any rate!" Bernard pointed. Indeed Tom could hardly help but be safe. Moby had obligingly wrecked the *Pied Piper* on the very reef that the Flat Island lighthouse was set to guard. A navy blue rescue launch was even now bringing him back to shore.

"No sign of Jill though!" said Uncle Fred. "If that villain has hurt her, I don't know what we'll do."

Just then a blue-jerseyed neighbor came running up. "What d'ye make of that?" he asked. Uncle Fred turned to look where he was pointing. From beyond one of the western rocks a column of smoke was rising into the afternoon sunshine. Uncle Fred adjusted the telescope.

"Someone's out there!" he gasped.

"It may be Jill!" cried Bernard.

"This," decided Uncle Fred, "is a case for Daisy May."

Within a few minutes men were clambering aboard a tractor and hurrying towards the western shore of the island.

At the end of the sandy beach was a long low cottage built of stone, with a thatched roof.

"That's where Daisy May lives!" Uncle Fred explained to Bernard with a grin.

"Why hasn't she any windows in her cottage?"

The reason was soon apparent.

Daisy May was an enormous rowing gig. The islanders went about launching her with the skill of long familiarity.

"This is the nearest thing we have to a real lifeboat," said Uncle Fred. "Men would always sooner trust to their sinews than to an engine when the storm winds are blowing. Besides, the oars help to balance her."

By crossing the island and launching a boat from the western shore they cut half an hour or more off the time that it would have taken to rescue Jill. Moreover, Bernard, who would otherwise have been left out of the adventures altogether, had the thrill of a trip in the Daisy May, "Which," as Uncle Fred declared, "is not a privilege given to every visitor."

"Hello," said Jill. "I was hoping you would hurry up and rescue me. I've been missing all the fun sitting out here."

"Missing all the fun!" said Bernard, indignantly. "I've been worried out of my mind."

"How sweet!" Jill dimpled, mischievously. "You should never worry about me. I can look after myself, you know."

"Grrh!" said Bernard.

He had his revenge later, however, for Auntie Su insisted on putting both the adventurers to bed early with a bowl of a ghastly concoction which she referred to as "nourishing gruel."

"I'm sure its the same stuff you use for hanging wallpaper!" muttered Tom.

Bernard sat out on the verandah watching the helicopter circling around the islands.

"They are searching for Mr. Danvers," said Uncle Fred. "The men have been back to look for his rubber dinghy, but it's missing. It looks as though he reached that at any rate. Finding him will be like looking for a needle in a haystack. There are many small caves in the Westward rock. He could hide in any one of them. Once darkness comes, he can get to the mainland."

"Will the dinghy get that far?"

"Well, it depends on how much gas he has. It will be a rough trip for him, but he'll make it."

"Tom is sorry that he lost your skiff."

"Yes, I know. I told him he can buy me a new one out of the reward money he gets!"

"Will there be a reward?"

"The police seem to think that there may be."

* *

By Saturday things were more or less back to normal. The newspapermen had gotten their story, and Jill had to sit by a fire on the beach to have her photograph taken as "the teen-age castaway."

Uncle Fred watched with satisfaction as the last launch left. "The island is never the same with a lot of foreigners tramping about," he said.

In the bungalow, Tom was putting the finishing

touches to his poster, and Bernard, with Bible and notepaper, was groaning over his sermon preparation.

"Nobody will come to listen anyhow!" he said.

Tom grinned. "You wait till they see my poster."

Jill was carefully pouring kerosene into the brass bowls of the lamps at the chapel. The glass cylinders which protected the wicks gleamed and shone.

"Do you have any thumbtacks?" asked Tom.

"Is that the poster?"

"Uh huh!"

"Let me see it!"

"Find some thumbtacks first."

"All right, I think there are some in the drawer."

Jill went out with Tom to the bulletin board, and together they tacked up the poster.

"Sunday Evening Service 6:30. Youth tells the Gospel," read Jill.

She stood looking at Tom's work admiringly with her head on one side.

"You're really quite professional, Tom."

"Do you like it?"

"Yes, I do."

"Good. I wanted to put in a cartoon of Bernard with a halo. But I thought it wasn't quite the thing."

"What's Bernard doing now?"

"Oh, going crazy over his sermon. He really *does* believe in it, doesn't he?"

"Yes," said Jill, and then she added, "Do you?"

Tom blushed.

"I'm too bad to be a Christian, Jill. Honest, I am. I'm just not the sort."

"When I became a Christian," said Jill, "my mother

118

told me that when you believe in Jesus, He wipes all your sins away just as if they were written on a blackboard and you sponged them off."

Tom sighed. "Mine won't rub off," he said.

At that moment Auntie Su rounded the end of the chapel.

"Ah, there you are, Jill," she said. "I've brought the hymnbook for you to practice."

Tom wandered off down the lane alone. The sound of the harmonium drifted out of the chapel door. A cow mooed at him over the hedge.

"It's all right for you," said Tom moodily, addressing the cow. "Your friends aren't always pestering you about religion."

* * *

Probably, under ordinary circumstances, no one would have turned up for the service at the chapel except Uncle Fred and Auntie Su. The events of the last few days had been far from ordinary, however.

"People are coming from all directions," said Auntie Su delightedly.

It was true enough. Almost everybody on the island had decided to hear the young man speak. After all, the trio of visitors had had such an adventure. Life was uneventful normally, and this was a novelty not to be missed.

By the time Bernard arrived at the chapel door, nervously clutching his Bible, the building seemed crowded. Being a sensible person, he realized the mixture of motives that had brought the congregation together. He also saw that it was too good an opportunity to miss.

119

Once the service began he found that his nervousness left him. He forgot himself altogether in a longing to tell the people about Jesus.

The text he chose was: "While we were yet sinners, Christ died for us." He found that he did not need his notes, but instead told the people sincerely how he had become a Christian himself.

Outside the window, dusk was falling. The kerosene lamps bathed the congregation in a yellow glow. Nobody fidgeted, and while Bernard was preaching, God's Holy Spirit told Tom that Jesus had died in his place on the Cross.

Walking home in the dusk together, with the "bosun" light flashing out over the still water, Tom cleared his throat and told Bernard that he now believed in Jesus for himself.

And Bernard thought to himself that he would rather have that happen than to have been the one who found the jewels that Moby stole.

17
Terror by Night

The asbestos bungalow where the two boys slept had two rooms in it, although only one was in use as a bedroom. The other was filled with junk of one kind and another. Old books were piled high in one corner. Several obsolete kerosene heaters, various pots and pans, and an army of trunks filled most of the room. A pair of old hip boots occupied the seat of a wicker chair. There were two old earthenware bowls and one pitcher. There was a grandfather clock, with its weights lying in the bottom of the case. There was a chest of old clothes, various pictures, and bric-a-brac of all kinds. Across one corner of the room hung a flowered curtain. It was suspended from a triangle of wood, thus making a kind of corner wardrobe.

Had anyone looked into the room late that Sunday evening he would have noticed that the toe of a boot was protruding from behind this curtain. Even that fact would not have aroused suspicion, however, because it was quite natural that a pair of boots should have been dumped in the corner. As a matter of fact, neither Tom nor Bernard glanced into the room at all. When they

121

came into the bungalow to go to bed, it was already beginning to get dark. They were both tired, so they only lit their candle, hurriedly undressed, and were soon ready for bed.

It was about 2 A.M. The moon had appeared from behind the clouds. Tom was snoring gently. Bernard turned over, muttered something in his sleep, and then lay still again. In the distance a night bird called eerily. The asbestos creaked slightly as the wind sighed against its corrugated walls.

The door of the junk room began to open very, very slowly. A floorboard creaked as the bulky figure of a man crept on tiptoe into the boys' bedroom. Pale moonlight filtering through the window showed the boys sound asleep. It also glinted upon the huge knife which had been part of Mr. Danvers's underwater swimming equipment, and which now glinted in his hand as he stooped over Tom's pillow. Suddenly he reached down and clapped a strong hand over Tom's mouth.

Tom woke up to find himself staring at the sharp point of the knife held about an inch above his eyes. With vivid awareness he noted its serrated edge. His consciousness seemed heightened. It was as though there was an eternity between one beat of his heart and the next. Months later the scene was still vividly imprinted upon his brain. He was scarcely able to breathe, but dared not protest because of the threat of the knife. His whole body went rigid with horror.

"Don't make a sound!" commanded Mr. Danvers. "Do you understand?"

Tom shut his eyes and opened them again. Mr. Danvers removed his hand, but not the knife.

122

Bernard awakened from deep sleep to hear Tom gently calling his name.

"What d'ye want?" he asked grumpily, and began to turn over in bed.

"You must wake up!" whispered Tom, urgently. "Mr. Danvers has kidnapped us!"

"What!" Bernard was suddenly wide awake.

"Lie still, Bernard, and do not make a sound," ordered Mr. Danvers. "If you shout, nobody is likely to hear you, but it will be so much the worse for Tom. Thanks to you two I've lost my jewels. The boat is a wreck, and I've been cooped up in a miserable cave for days. I haven't had a square meal since my emergency rations ran out. I'm a desperate man, so you had better do exactly as I tell you."

Roughly Mr. Danvers pulled the bedclothes off Tom. "Get up," he ordered sharply.

Prodded by the ugly point of the knife, Tom got out of bed. He hoped Mr. Danvers was bluffing, but he was by no means sure. With several days' growth of beard on his chin, and a fierce look of desperation in his eyes, Mr. Danvers no longer looked the smooth professional man he had seemed. Tom noticed that Mr. Danvers was not in the frogman's outfit. From somewhere he had obtained seaman's trousers, and a gray turtleneck jersey. He wore heavy boots on his feet.

"I always knew my first aid kit would come in handy," joked Mr. Danvers, grimly. "Take this tape and stick it over Bernard's mouth."

Reluctantly Tom did as he was told. Bernard had no choice but to submit.

"Sorry, old chap!" whispered Tom.

123

"Now tie his hands and feet." Danvers produced a length of strong picture cord.

Tom had some idea that he might be able to tie a granny knot which Bernard could work loose, but Danvers saw to it that the job was well done. Tom was forced to tie Bernard's ankles a second time before Danvers was satisfied that the knots were good enough.

"It will take you a while to wriggle out of that!" he declared.

Then he forced Tom to lie down again while he fastened a second length of tape over his mouth. It felt horrible. Tom's eyes were glinting with fury, but there was nothing he could do. Mr. Danvers was master of the situation.

"Now get up, and get dressed. You are coming with me. Don't touch that gag unless you want me to get nasty." As Tom got dressed, Danvers stood over Bernard and gave him instructions.

"Now listen to me, Bernard. Tom is my hostage. When I am gone you will doubtless try to get free. It should take you some time. However, when you have done so, you can take a message from me to your uncle. Tell him I am taking his boat, and I am taking Tom. Is that clear? If he tells the police and I find that I am pursued. . . . Well, Tom will be dead before they get me. Do you understand? If he has any sense he'll keep quiet and give me time to get ashore. Then after a few days I will set Tom free. And I may even tell him where your uncle can find his boat. Tell him I'm desperate, and I mean what I say. If I'm caught, I'll get a long sentence anyhow so it won't trouble me to rub Tom out if I have to."

By this time Tom was dressed, and Danvers seized him by the arm.

"Tell Bernard that I mean what I say," ordered Danvers, fiercely. He screwed Tom's arm behind his back. Tom, gagged as he was, couldn't say anything. Danvers twisted harder. Tom felt as though his arm was being wrenched out of the socket. He squealed desperately down his nostrils. Bernard's eyes had tears in them, and he struggled desperately to get free, but without success.

Danvers laughed quietly.

"Yes, I mean it," he said, and twisted Tom's arm again. "Do you understand?"

Bernard nodded frantically.

"Good! Then let's be going, Tom. Don't try and run for it or there will be trouble!"

At knife-point Tom left the bungalow. Danvers was on his heels. The air was cold, and Tom's teeth felt as though they wanted to chatter. The tape across his lips was hurting him. He longed to tear it off, but he dared not do so. Danvers was so close that he could hear his breathing.

"Down to the beach," he whispered. Silently they hurried down through the fields towards the boats lying at anchor in the bay. The "bosun" light flashed in the distance.

Bernard found that it was far worse to be tied up than he had ever imagined. His wrists were painful, and he had to fight against a tendency to kick and struggle with panic.

"How can I get free?" He forced himself to lie still and think carefully. "I must find something sharp."

125

Mentally he checked through his possessions. He remembered his razor. He had not unpacked this, for, truth to tell, he had no real need of it yet. An aunt had given it to him at Christmas time—it was really a joke on her part—but Bernard was secretly rather pleased to own a razor. It made him feel more grown up than he really was. About once a month his chin produced enough down to justify a shave. He had brought the razor with him, but, at the last moment, dreading Tom's sense of humor, he had not unpacked it.

The razor was still in his suitcase, but how was he to get to it? He rolled from the bed, bringing the bedclothes down on top of him. With his hands tied behind his back it was difficult to get the suitcase unlocked, but eventually he succeeded in doing so. He was able to grope for the razor in its plastic container. Once the razor was in his hands he managed to unscrew it without difficulty. Gingerly he extracted the blade. He sat up on the floor and inserted the blade in a crack in the floorboards. He was terrified of breaking the slender blade. He had others in a dispenser, but there was not a second to lose.

Patiently Bernard sawed away. The cord was not thick, and much more quickly than he could have hoped, the cords were cut. Eagerly he snatched the tape from his lips, and opened his mouth to call for help. Then he shut it again, and instead of calling, he began to cut his legs free.

"What's the use of shouting?" he thought to himself. "Uncle Fred will be terribly upset, but with Tom held hostage there is nothing that he can do."

Bernard knew that even the police seemed helpless in

the case of a hijacking. Kidnappers seemed to have everything in their favor. Once Danvers reached the boat it would be too late to do anything.

Perhaps it was too late already.

18
Capture

The journey down through the moonlit fields seemed utterly unreal to Tom. Shock had set in, and his brain refused to admit the evidence of his senses. He moved as in a dream. He had read about kidnappings in the newspapers. But he had never realized how the victims felt. It all seemed so unfair. This sort of thing only happened to famous and important people. His foot dislodged a stone as they clambered up the steps of a stile to get over a fence. Moby cursed him under his breath. Tom could tell that the man was panicky, and it was this that made Tom even more frightened. There was no telling what might happen if Moby was cornered.

Now they had reached the wooden ladder leading down to the beach. Tom wondered whether he could make a break for it, but Danvers was close behind him. He was bigger, stronger, and quicker than Tom.

They trudged across the beach. The sand scrunched beneath their feet. The waves lapped gently on the shore.

"Untie the rope." Moby pointed to the mooring line

of the skiff. He stood over Tom as the boy obediently stooped and began to undo the reef knot.

* * *

Bernard, having freed himself, hurriedly pulled on a sweater and jeans. He slipped into his sneakers, and snatched up his slingshot and lead pellets. He ran out of the bungalow, and down the path which led towards the beach. As far as possible he kept in the shadows. His sneakers made no sound on the grass as he ran.

At the top of the wooden steps leading to the beach stood an old hut which Uncle Fred usually kept locked. It contained some old nets, a rusty anchor or two, and Uncle Fred's pride and joy, a large belt-operated circular saw which he used for cutting driftwood.

The shadow of this hut gave Bernard a vantage point for observing the scene on the beach. Tom and Moby were at no great distance from him, although of course they were some twenty feet lower. Standing in the shadows on the cliff top Bernard had an ideal position from which to launch his secret attack.

Tom was unfastening the rope. Mr. Danvers stood over him with his back towards the wooden ladder. Bernard could even hear him whisper, "Hurry up, can't you!"

Bernard fitted one of the lead pellets into his slingshot and took careful aim. The first shot missed the man completely and kicked up a little spurt of sand as the heavy pellet buried itself in the soft beach.

Mr. Danvers was immediately on the alert.

"What was that?" He swung towards the shore and searched the cliff top with a suspicious gaze. He saw nothing, however. The night remained calm and still.

130

Tom of course knew exactly what the noise was and his heart had given a great leap of joy. They would do for old Moby yet! he thought to himself with satisfaction. Good old Bernard, there was a chance of escape after all. Many times he had heard the "zip" of Bernard's slingshot elastic, and he knew his friend was a good shot.

Tom stooped to the boat and gave it a push. The noise of the gravel under its keel would mask any other sound Bernard made.

Bernard's first shot had given him a good idea of the range. The second pellet caught Moby fair and square between the shoulder blades. It did not penetrate his clothing, but it had a powerful impact all the same, and Moby obviously thought that he had been shot. He let out a roar and jumped in the air, frenziedly trying to clutch at the imagined wound.

Tom, who had been waiting for this moment, seized his opportunity. Leaving the boat, he raced across the beach towards the ladder as fast as his feet would carry him. Bernard, watching anxiously from above, saw Moby turn and begin to chase after Tom.

On the track at school, Tom could make good time. But running on the beach was quite different. The further he got towards the ladder, the more fine and powdery the sand became. Here and there were granite boulders threatening to trip him. The fickle moonlight cast shadows which sometimes made these boulders seem larger than they were. Tom's feet sank into the sand. His breath came in short gasps.

"Faster, faster!" Tom's brain was urging him forward. He longed to glance behind to see how close

Moby was, but he knew that he must concentrate every effort upon reaching the ladder.

It seemed to him that he was running in slow motion. His calf muscles ached, and his lungs were bursting. He could feel the blood pounding in his temples.

After the first shout of pain and fear Moby had made no further sound. He knew that he must catch Tom before Tom could reach the ladder which led from the beach. Grimly he spurted after Tom. The sand made it even harder for him, as he was far heavier. Nevertheless he was strong and in good condition despite his weight. The distance between the two runners began to narrow.

"Wang!" Bernard's third and fourth shots had been misses. The fifth caught Moby on the kneecap. He stumbled, and then clutching the injured knee jumped up and down on one leg.

In any ordinary circumstances he would have emitted a howl of pain and rage, but he did not dare to do so. He made a grotesque figure as he capered on the sand. However, pain seemed to spur him on, and the next moment he was running faster than ever.

The brief delay gave Tom enough time to reach the bottom of the wooden steps. Thankfully he began to climb. He was as agile as a monkey, and in a moment he had reached the top. It was not a second too soon.

"Here!" gasped Bernard. "Help me!"

A net had been hung out over an old oar near the top of the wooden steps. Bernard had bundled this into his arms. As Moby came up the ladder they flung the net over him, entangling him.

"Look what we've caught!" shouted Bernard, gleefully. His triumph was short-lived however. Despite the net, Moby managed to make it to the top of the ladder. He fell heavily on the grass, but even so he still kept hold of the sharp knife. The strands of the net began to part as he slashed at the twine from inside the net.

Tom had torn the tape from his lips.

"Go for his legs!" he cried.

The three of them struggled in a frenzied heap at the top of the cliff.

Moby had the strength of a wrestler. He kicked violently with his legs.

"We'll never hold him!" gasped Bernard.

"Run for it then," agreed Tom.

Giving up the unequal struggle the boys fled in opposite directions. Bernard was not quick enough however. Moby flung himself upon him as he turned to run and the two of them went down again. On his own Bernard had no chance at all. Moby's weight pinioned him to the ground.

"Come back, Tom!" ordered Moby. "It will be the worse for your friend Bernard if you don't."

Tom halted in his tracks, and reluctantly returned. Bernard could see the evil glint in Moby's eyes.

"He means it, Tom, I'm afraid. . . ."

"Yes, I do mean it," cried Mr. Danvers triumphantly.

"Yes," said a strange voice, grimly, "I really think you do."

Suddenly Moby's wrist was seized in an iron grip from behind. He dropped the knife, squealing in sudden anguish.

A man's shape loomed behind him, and the voice went on, "Now if you will just come along quietly with me, sir, there are a few questions I would like to ask you."

Moby seemed to have shrunk like a pricked balloon.

"It was just a game, officer. . . ." he began, lamely.

"No doubt, sir," replied the plain-clothes policeman, phlegmatically. "However if you will return to the house with me it will make things easier all around."

All the fight seemed to have left Moby. He slunk up the field with the policeman's hand on his arm. Another man also appeared and took charge of the boys.

"Just like the movies," said Tom, grinning with satisfaction. "Of course we would have managed him alone, you know!"

"I dare say," agreed the man.

"Don't be silly, Tom," scolded Bernard. "We wouldn't have stood a chance, and you know it. I've never been more thankful in my life. But where did you come from?"

"We've been keeping watch from your uncle's shed. The police aren't as stupid as all that, you know. We thought this man might still be on the Island. In any case it was normal routine to keep a watch for a day or two."

A sudden thought struck Tom.

"Bernard?"

"Yes?"

"You don't think your aunt will want me to take any more of that ghastly gruel, do you?"

19
No More Adventures

"Now listen to me, you three," said Auntie Su sternly, "for the rest of this vacation there are to be no more adventures. Your Uncle Fred and I have never had such frights as we have had these last few days. If there is any more of it we shall have to send you packing."

"Oh, Auntie, you wouldn't," begged Jill.

"Wouldn't I just," said Auntie Su. "Try me and see!"

An efficient-looking launch had come to the wharf in the light of early dawn, and Mr. Danvers, closely escorted by burly men, had been spirited away. Auntie Su had been dissuaded from dishing out beneficial medicines, and Uncle Fred had finally convinced her that perhaps the youngsters would not rest even if they were sent back to bed. So she had made an early breakfast instead, and the boys had told their story again and again.

"Well," said Tom, sadly, "no more adventures then. . . . Auntie Su, will you teach me how to crochet?"

"Well Tom. . . ." she began. Then she stopped. "You young monkey, you're teasing, aren't you!"

"Auntie Su, what could make you think such a thing!"

"I know what we'll do," said Uncle Fred. "We've all had a rough time. Let's have a celebration. We'll go for a picnic."

"Where shall we go?"

"I'll take you out to one of the uninhabited islands. There's a crate of root beer we've been keeping, and we'll light a fire and cook something. Then shrimps to follow. . . . How does that sound?"

"Sounds just right to me!" cried Bernard.

"And me!" said Tom.

"Me, too!" added Jill.

Auntie Su nodded her approval. "After all," she said, "nothing could possibly happen on a picnic."

Tom nudged Bernard and gave him a broad wink.